Frogley/STRIPLING/1

Frogley/STRIPLING/2

A Book of Mormon Historical Fiction

TABLE OF CONTENTS:

STRIPLING:
By Craig R. Frogley

STRIPLING

By Craig R. Frogley

PREFACE:

Please, before reading this work of fiction, re-read Alma chapters 24, 25, 27, 53, 56-58 through Helaman 3. Knowing the scriptural account will allow this fiction to come alive and prevent conflating imagined events and people as if they were true. But, that said, keep your eyes and heart open for possible symbols and modern applications of this true to life story.

For example, the word used by Helaman to describe the young warriors from the converted Lamanite families now called "people of Ammon," was "stripling." Though we don't have the original Hebrew or reformed Egyptian word from the gold plates, when it is searched in an English-Hebrew dictionary the finding is עֶלֶם. When searched in the Bible that word is used twice to describe an unmarried youth of marriageable or childbearing age. According to the online Jewish Encyclopedia that age is between puberty which culminates at age fourteen and age twenty after which he would be considered cursed by God for not finding a woman that would marry him. [1]

---

[1] According to calculations by John Tvedtnes they were between 21-26
https://www.churchofjesuschrist.org/study/ensign/1992/09/i-have-a-question/what-were-the-ages-of-helamans-stripling-warriors?lang=eng

In 1 Samuel 2:20 "stripling" is used to refer to a lad or young man sent on a secret errand. Also, in 1 Samuel 17:56 it is used to refer to young David who had just surprised all of Israel and the Phillistines by killing Goliath. Again, we see a willing and prepared youth used by the Lord as a secret weapon in the salvation of Israel. Interestingly, the origin of the Hebrew word used, is a primitive root meaning "conceal" or a "secret thing." Was Helaman creating a play on the Hebrew word for "stripling" since Helaman's striplings turn out to be the Lord's secret weapon in this precarious war with the dissenters, Amalakiah and his brother Ammoron, who had manipulated the Lamanites into a war for "world domination?" In a modern-day war against the actual secret combination vying for world domination, a modern prophet has likewise called for a youth battalion. [2]

Timeline:[3]

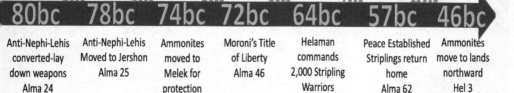

	2Yrs	5Yrs	1Yrs	8Yrs	7Yrs	11Yrs	
80bc	78bc	74bc	72bc	64bc	57bc	46bc	
Anti-Nephi-Lehis converted-lay down weapons Alma 24	Anti-Nephi-Lehis Moved to Jershon Alma 25	Ammonites moved to Melek for protection Alma 35	Moroni's Title of Liberty Alma 46	Helaman commands 2,000 Stripling Warriors Alma 53	Peace Established Striplings return home Alma 62	Ammonites move to lands northward Hel 3	

President Russell M. Nelson: Ensign
http://www.bmaf.org/node/339

A timeline is not as fixed and predictable as one might think even though the Nephites were regular in noting what year it was relative to either their departure from Jerusalem, year of the reign of the judges, or the sign given of the birth of Christ. Matching that to our calendar is somewhat problematic because of calendar differences, but an effort has been made to approximate the passage of years. Sam's age is noted as age five at the death of his father. He is eighteen when the "stripling" plan is accepted. About seven years passes before they return home so he must be twenty-five.[4]

---

[4] https://virtualscriptures.org/book-of-mormon-map/

INTRODUCTION

The stars danced in the black fabric of eternity like fading coals in the night's dinner fire. Mother lovingly tucked me into bed saying again, "Someday you will be a great warrior like your father, Samy." There just was no one like my father. Even though I was only five at the time, I could tell that he was better than any other in the world. Before Brother Ammon came, Father was gone a lot because he was the best warrior in all the land of Jerusalem. At least, that is what all my friends told me and my mom, too.

Some things began to change when father brought Brother Ammon to our home. I liked him right away, even though I found out later that he was a Nephite. He taught me how to shoot a sling at a target. He could hit his every time and worked with me until I could too. He talked for a long time, over many days with my parents. They would tell me stories later about Adam and Eve and the great creator God, Jehovah, who would come to earth as Jesus, to heal and save all the people. It made me feel like a warm blanket during a cold night. Brother Ammon would even tell me stories and play with me when he didn't have to go save someone. All our people seemed to really love him; I know that I did almost as much as my giant father.

After Brother Ammon taught my parents and me, things changed a lot. Dad was home more, and I never saw him with his sword, cimeter, or axe.

He stopped teaching me to use my little sword, so we hiked a lot and played and swam together. We even started farming as a family which eventually included my two little sisters. At the time, I didn't really understand what had happened, but I felt a great difference, a peace, in our home and even in our village.

But then, things seemed to get very tense. I overheard mother and Father talking about going to meet someone. Father said he had to go without mother and would probably not come back. "Oh Aaron, what…" I heard her say before silence bound her tongue. I watched tears fall from mother's eyes as they hugged for a long time until I couldn't stand it any longer and ran to join the family embrace. All of us three children seemed to come out of hiding together as we merged into one big loving circle, especially with mother's growing belly. Father took me aside, kneeling before me, taking me by the shoulders, and seriously looked me in the eye and said, "Sam, though you are very young, I need your oath that you will obey your mother with exactness, for Papa is going to go and keep his." I nodded and watched as he left us, carrying only his prayer cloth. I never saw him again even though I have tried to keep his image in my mind. I don't remember all that was going on, but we moved to a new land. There were many of us and we liked the new land, but I missed my father more than my sisters and new little brother who never got to meet him. Our lives would suffer many more upheavals and joys in the course of my days.

I write this from the land northward many years following my father's departure and entrance into the world of spirits. I am of no more consequence than any of the other of my brethren, yet I have seen the goodness of God throughout my life. There are two things that weigh upon my mind and press me to engrave these things: First, in retrospect I can see how some choices act like tiny hinges upon which the great results of life turn. Choosing to believe in God and then choosing to follow the doctrine of Christ was not an easy decision for my people, it was not one that Korihor would have found logical and one for which many gave their lives. Nor was it one where the first step could have ever predicted the latter results. Knowing the end from the beginning, before making a choice is not part of productive mortality even in the guise of trying to avoid deception. The incremental evidence only comes to those willing to take a risk by acting on a chosen belief as if it were reality until the fruits of time manifest the goodness of the choice and its part of the Greater Truths of eternity. Some may point to the death of my father and say that his choice led to a disastrous result. But, unlike the Lamanites who also have died, but without having chosen the covenant path, he died saving lives, happy with the deep fulfillment that only comes from divine sources.

Second, I also write to testify, as you will see, that God can do anything with the least of us, if we are willing to let him make the incremental transformations needed at the unforeseeable moments of doing the hard things, He will require of those who want to contribute. Because hard things are simply the accumulation of many small daily investments in obedience to God's commandments, hard things are easy things done late when they must be done all at once. The grace by which we are saved can only flow into our lives by allowing it to flow out of our lives in bettering our fellowman. He transforms us better by working through us than by working on us.

CHAPTER 1: The Seed of Faith (About 77 BC)

On one hot sunny day while we were crossing the wilderness, during the move of our people to the lush new land called Jershon, I remember that our little fatherless family was at the end of the long column of people. Though one of my sisters had gone ahead following one of her friends, suddenly I saw her standing trembling-still in a clump of rocks where some had apparently stopped for their noon meal. As I caught up to her, I looked to follow her gaze and also froze seeing the viper nest in the barren rocks that now separated us from the rest of our people. We stood frozen in fear as the snakes slithered and coiled in front of us beneath the blazing sun. Her little whimper awakened me, and I snatched her back away from the serpents. To join the others, we were going to have to pass through the nest that had become active after everyone had walked through, and the heat of the day had invited them from their dens. As we stood watching the others in the distance through the rocks, our little family and those now coiled vipers, my mother came forward. Suddenly, I felt something abruptly different, a great peace filled me…I looked up to my mother who now stood head bowed. I didn't understand, but as she opened her eyes, she said, "fear not my little ones. The great Jehovah is with us. Hold to me and we will pass through unharmed."

In contrast to my feeling, I couldn't believe what I was hearing. Just the week before, I had seen the death sickness in one of the villagers who had been struck by a viper. It was awful so I held tightly to mother and my little sister as we walked towards the nest and passed right through those towering rocks and vicious snakes. I could hear the hissing and see the coiled serpents with beady eyes and slithering tongues, but mother encouraged us to look forward and trust. I was amazed and began to praise the great power of my mother when she said, "Sam, our God, who is our Father, continues with us, never fear, obey with exactness, and see Him work His miracles." I never forgot the feeling that pierced deeply into my little heart that day! For years I had felt so abandoned, vulnerable, without father. I knew then that I was not alone for I could always look to my mother who helped me trust in God as my father and protector.

Years after we had settled in Jershon, at twelve years of age, I heard a rumor spreading throughout the several villages about the man who had killed "our best warrior" years ago. I knew who the best of those warriors was, but how could someone be boasting about killing. Mother had taught me about the sacredness of life. Though only twelve, I found the fight inside me was stronger than I had ever known. I wanted to find this braggart and hurt him. Had he killed my father?? One day while I was tilling in the dark moist soil of our field, one of my friends ran to tell me that the very man, named Lahentah, was passing through our village preaching. That really confused me. How could this be? The only preachers I knew were our elders and Brother Ammon.

That evening our whole family went to hear this preacher—this murdering preacher! From our place in the middle front of our people I could see Lahentah's eyes searching the crowd in the dancing of the firelight. Our village father welcomed us and bowed and gave "thanks to the great God of Ammon, and Aaron, even Jesus Christ." Then, when Lahentah began to tell his story, I listened carefully but glared showing hatred, until my mother saw my eyes. "Samy," she whispered, "You cannot hear the Holy Spirit in your heart with what is on your face!" Then I heard Lahentah say, "In the years before we moved here to Jershon, I had been with the Amalakite-Lamanite-Amulonite confederation army. We all despised what the Nephite missionaries were creating in our land. We were ordered to war against them in order to stop this traitorous Nephite incursion into our nation. As we took to the battlefield, we could see the gathering of those deceived converts with none other than our greatest warrior, captain Aaron, standing at their head. When I saw him, I recognized him as the one who had killed my brother at the behest of king Lamoni long before the Nephite missionaries had come.

How had he, since, been fooled by those conspiring Nephites? As we attacked, I charged straight towards him. To my surprise, he knelt, then fell prostrate on the ground. Was he cowering before me? I praised the Great Spirit and with one blow, ended his cowardly conspiring life. But I was immediately stricken with wonder, there was no fight, and others around us were dying in the same manner—prostrate and submissive. Had we been lied to by our Amalekite captains? Though they had been deceived by the preaching of the Nephite missionaries, these were still our people of Laman! Perhaps, those Amalekites were setting us against each other. The thought stopped me, and I looked back at that warrior champion…what? Wait, was that movement? Was he not yet dead? I gently lifted his head as he spoke, lying on his back. In his dying breath, he bore witness of Jesus Christ and told me that he forgave me and loved me, then he sighed his last and closed his eyes. He was a true warrior with a weapon I had never encountered before that pierced my heart. I would have traded places with him if I could, to somehow save his life. The desire to never kill again hit me with indescribable force. My sword burned in my hand, I threw it far, and prostrated myself before this Jesus Christ who filled me with His love. How could THIS be? I, who had killed one of His… I was filled with a sense of forgiveness and intense love. This great warrior saved my eternal life by his example, dying witness, and loving forgiveness. I will never forget the love I felt coming from his eyes that spread throughout my soul as I came to feel

Jesus! I have come today, after all these years to plead for your forgiveness

and to help you cope with his death. I know that his family is here today. I

would give my life to bring him back, but since I have not that power, I have

given it to Christ to use as He chooses."

Though just a young boy, I remember feeling ashamed, yet at the

same time, I was filled with pride for my faithful warrior father. I determined

then and there that I, too, would learn to use that new weapon that pierces

hearts and saves lives. Mother pulled me close, seeing the great change

come over me. At that moment, I heard something and looked up. There

standing over me was Lahentah, he knelt before us, bowed, and sobbed with

hands out inviting us to him. I entered his embrace as we wept

together…mother followed, then my sisters and six-year-old brother. I would

never again be the same.

Little Aaron broke the silence, "Mother, you have taught me to forgive

the bad men who killed my father as he kept his oath to never kill. But if this

is the man who killed father, why does he feel so good?" We all laughed and

then stopped as Mother, my sweet and faithful mother, spoke softly, "Aaron,

the great Father in Heaven works in powerful ways to save His children here

on Mother Earth. He will send His Son to give His life to save us all, so He

asks that we give our lives to save each other. Your father, for whom you are named, followed Jesus and now Lahentah is doing the same by giving his life to help other children of the Great Heavenly Father change their lives too." I don't know if Aaron understood, but my heart was again pierced. I knew what I would do with my life. I loved my mother and couldn't doubt that she knew and trusted Jesus. I was reminded that if my mother had come to completely trust him then, so would I.

CHAPTER 2: Korihor See Alma 30 (74 BC)

Over the next few years, Lahentah stayed in the village and became a good friend to the family. He helped with our fields, often ate at our table, and loved each of us like father certainly would have done. I learned how to be a man from the times we spent and worked together. Little Aaron was growing fast and at age twelve, he could work right along side us. During the last couple of years, we had to work long days to provide food for our brethren, the Nephites. They protected us from Lamanites and Nephite dissenters thus enabling our brethren to be faithful to the oath that Father had died to keep.

One such dissenter named Korihor, who had begun his ministry in Zarahemla, entered our land preaching as he had done elsewhere. I had never heard such reasoning before and found myself intrigued, though at first, I felt a dark presence about him. He was refined of speech and a large mighty man. Curiosity led me to first listen and then engage him. Because I was young, barely past my coming of age, he gave my questions little attention. He seemed more interested in the young women, and they apparently found him alluring.

Looking up at him standing on a raised stone, I tried again meekly asking, "Excuse me sir, but I was wondering why you say that we cannot know of things we cannot see. I do know of things such as love, and peace, yet I cannot see them. Can you help me understand your meaning?"

"Boy, you are too young to understand the finer reasoning and have been deceived by those who would get gain from your ignorance!"

Meekly, I stood to my full height and stepped up onto the rock near him. Though he was large of stature and very comely, I towered over him, being of the stature of my father and large for my age, and replied firmly, "That didn't help me understand, Sir. Our priests get no gain from their preaching, we pay them nothing, so perhaps you are misinformed. But what you say, certainly has nothing to do with knowing beyond our five senses. I did not see the power my mother wielded when she chased the serpents from before us, Nor the power that changed the heart of the warrior, Lahentah, as my father testified of Christ to him, I boldly asserted, "I have felt such power. I have seen it work and even used it to gain understanding of the Holy Scriptures that you mock."

It surprised me to see the young women change their demeanor. They had been flirting with Korihor but now disenchantedly gazed upon him perhaps realizing truth as it compared to his negative logic and overt accusations. Korihor began to anger as the young women started to turn away in disdain, finally seeing the "real Korihor" for the first time. When he threateningly stepped towards me, a group of adults stepped out from the crowd and joined me. I was filled with a sweet sense of companionship in their support. At first, Korihor backed away, feeling suddenly isolated, but then lunged, ready to strike. At that moment, several other men seized him, bound him and we carried him, struggling and cursing, to Ammon, our High Priest. I was there when Korihor was banished, then taken out of our land of Melek. Eventually, he was taken before the high priest, Alma, in the land of Zarahemla. Sometimes it is only the passage of time, with its natural consequences, that reveals the truth of both an argument and the man who wields it. Once rejected, he sought sustenance from the wicked Zoramites, who eventually trampled him to death. I found this personally instructive since he suffered the very consequences of the doctrine he had preached. Results reveal truth!

Korihor's demise was but a preview of what the Zoramites sought to do to those of their community who were converted by the prophet, Alma, because his teachings ruined their priestcraft. Alma sent them immediately to live with us in Jershon. But the Zoramites would have none of it and so joined with the seemingly innumerable hosts of the Lamanites to seek revenge. They marshaled for war against us in order to destroy their converted countrymen. Something had to be done since all our warriors were under the oath and had buried their weapons. After consulting with the government, the elders decided to move our entire community to a location far from the border with the Lamanites.

The sudden move of our entire community, several villages, was brought on by this Zoramite anger that united them with the Lamanites, as enemies to the people of God. The Nephite armies had moved into our villages to protect the land from the invasion, so we gathered what we could, leaving provisions for the army, and left hastily. Our destination was Melek, a beautiful city at the foot of a high mountain range along a small but lovely river where the people were friendly and accepting. I would later learn that Alma had been recently preaching amongst them finding them humble and teachable. They too lived Jehovah's teachings making our transition less traumatic.

During the long march first northward and then southwest through the great central valley, we found it exhausting but no one complained as we assisted the children and elderly. Little Naomi plopped down right in front of me as I turned from lifting Sister Sarah's pack from her bent aging back. I almost tripped over her as I added the pack to mine. "Naomi, I am sorry, are you alright?"

"No, I not alright, I hungry and tired!" I lifted her into my arms and reached into my pocket to retrieve the fruit I had saved for just this occasion.

"I have a surprise for you, Naomi, close your eyes." She squealed in delight as I cut a slice and placed it in her mouth.

Leaving our Jershon seashore was the most difficult for me as I missed the roar of the surf alternating with the peaceful lapping of the waves. As we marched together passing Zarahemla and the river Sidon, I marveled at the beauty of the wide mountain encircled valley. The sun was setting as we followed the river into Melek and safety. We couldn't have known that we would never return to what had become our homeland.   With the defeat of Zarahemna (74 BC) and his Zoramite-Lamanite confederation came peace to our new home as Nephite warriors returned. The long days working to improve the city to accommodate so many of us, made it difficult to spend much time with my friends, especially Lilly. Memories of the sea beaconed as we had loved long walks in the surf as children, but the surrounding mountain beauty and cool river called much the same. Being together made for heaven on earth for me, but I wondered if she shared those feelings. I could talk to my friends but to wonder such things out loud seemed frightening and increasingly important to me. One hot day, as we left to swim in the cool waters with a group of friends, her mother called, "Lilly, Lilly, I am sorry to interrupt…but I bring news everyone needs to hear. I returned from speaking with the King. He was stern in warning us that the Nephite-Lamanite war was getting more dangerous and would soon impact our lives even more." To our young minds, we could hardly imagine anything worse than having to move again.

CHAPTER 3: Lilly

A few of us friends were returning through the orchard from working together to help a widow in the village, a while later. It was during these youth work projects that I really began to want to spend more and more time with Lilly. She would later tell me why her family became involved in our friendship.

"Lilly," Abish called from across the orchard.

Lilly came running, "Here, mother, what do you need?"

"Lilly, who is that boy that I have seen you with over the summer? Isn't that who you were with just now?"

"His name is Sam, but don't worry mother, we are many friends together. Sam is one of the boys from the other side of the village. We all used to play together at the beach in our old home. We see each other whenever we do a youth service for someone in the village. I think that he likes me but...anyway, I think that you would like him, he is so nice and works harder than all the other boys together!"

"Lilly, do you like him?

Yes, Momma but, you know that I am betrothed to Luram.

That is true, Lilly, but I have a feeling that I would like to meet him. Perhaps we could invite his family for a meal on the Sabbath."

"Momma, I would love that but is it right...with Luram and all?

If we invite his family, we will be doing what we have always done in befriending the other members of our community. It is growing and we don't know everyone. This doesn't have to be about you two.

Ok, Momma, I would love that. He makes me feel very special when am around him, even just working. I have not met his family yet, but I will ask him. He is very nice, but he doesn't have a father anymore."

"All the more reason. We will plan on it."

Sam brought his family that Sabbath, and it was like we had all been friends forever.

After dinner and cleanup, once we were alone in the cool of the evening, Sam asked, "Lilly, was your mother really a servant to king Lamoni" He is a legend among our people! Do you know him personally?"

"Mother talks about him and the queen quite often. She really loves them. The queen passed into the world of spirits last year, so mother has invited him to dine with us more frequently. Yes, we are all quite close."

What I didn't tell him was that Luram, son of King Lamoni, was also very close to our family. Our fathers had agreed when we were children, that we would become betrothed as we both came of age. Having Sam in our group of friends only complicated things for me. I knew that he liked me and would sometimes try to get between Luram and me.

Over the next few years, Sam and I saw a lot of each other until, as I turned sixteen, I had a dream. I was in a beautiful meadow with a waterfall. It was an ideal and peaceful place. I stood at the foot of the waterfall loving all around me but wondering why I was there. stepping from underneath, the waterfall came Sam, tall with his long dark hair pulled back and wet from his passage and his muscles glistening with water. I wanted to go to him but knew that Luram nor my parents would be pleased. As I hesitated, his eyes locked on mine and I knew his thoughts—just then Luram joined me, stepping from the forest. He must have seen what passed between Sam and me and so spoke, "Lilly, it is God's will that you go to him. I love you, but you have been chosen for another. I hesitated to tell you but can see that Father has bound you two, in spite of my hesitancy. He turned to peer into the trees from whence he came. Was there someone waiting for him there?" Then a voice spoke above us, "Lilly, I have a great work for each of you that requires that you turn your whole heart to my servant, Sam." As I broke my gaze from Luram to once again lock eyes with Sam, I woke with the greatest joy! But how would I tell my father and Luram? Had God shown the same dream to Luram or Sam?

After many days of fasting and prayer, avoiding people so I could be alone, I began to hope that God had already inspired our parents, so they would end our betrothal. But one day mother called with a worry in her voice.

"Lilly, I must have your help, there is much to do in the orchard. Can you plan on spending the day with your sisters and me?"

"Mother, I will do as you say, but I must speak with you before my heart bursts."

"Lilly, what is it, my darling?"

I began slowly. The words I needed seemed to come unplanned, "Mother, do you remember telling us about your vision of your father that converted you to Jesus and gave you your name?"

"Yes, of course, Lilly, it was a most singular spiritual experience. He taught me from the world of Spirits. Why do you ask?"

"Well," I started slowly, almost too quietly, "I, too, have had a vision, a most joyous and vivid dream. I think that it was from my father, as well. But how do I know for certain?"

"Lilly, only the Spirit can verify such things, but perhaps I can help. Could you share it with me?"

I told mother every detail and again felt that same joy I had as my eyes locked with Sam's. I knew in my heart that it was right that I was chosen for Sam but couldn't convince my mind that I could hurt Luram by telling him. I needed mother's wisdom and guidance. We sat watching each other for a long time.

Finally, she spoke, "Lilly, perhaps the timing of what I was going to tell you will allow things to work themselves out without all the awkwardness this would create between our families. I have come from our dear friend and former king Lamoni. He has shared that there is increasing tension with the Lamanites. We must be ready; the armies will need our food. If there is a need, both Luram and Sam may be taken away into God's hands. For now, say nothing to either of them. I will talk to your father, and we will pray to know what to do."

Mother was right, I needed to trust my Father in Heaven. The next day, we were all together to help with a widow's garden. As I greeted both Sam and Luram, I could tell something had changed. Could they feel it? I wanted so to speak what was in my heart. I loved both but knew that God's wisdom must prevail. Luram and I had grown up knowing that someday we would be raising a family together. It had colored everything we talked about and planned. My attraction to Sam had filled me with a mixture of joy and guilt. It, too, had colored our conversations. He had been more forward, so I used humor to dismiss some of his overtures. But I found him more connected with Father than Luram. His faith seemed so powerful! Now I understood, God had a work for Sam to do. What would it be, and what would be my part in it with him? What would Luram do? In my dream, was there another he was attracted to like I was to Sam? Could that be? If so,

how would I take it, once I know who It was?

Luram and I found ourselves carrying a large basket together out to

the compost hole. Since we were alone, I wanted to ask him about "her" but

kept my promise to mother… to wait. But then he spoke,

"Lilly, I need to speak to you."

"But Luram, I laughed, you are speaking to me now. Is there

something more of great importance?"

He didn't laugh but became very serious, "Lilly, do you still feel

committed to our betrothal? We were children when our fathers made the

decision for us. How do you feel now?"

I am certain that I looked almost shocked, and my heart was racing,

but what could I say that would make it safe for him to reveal his heart

without revealing mine first? "Luram, I think that you know that I have been

committed to our betrothal, but I don't want you to feel forced into anything.

There must be good reason for you to ask."

"Lilly, I do not want to force you into marriage with me either. I have

been thinking the last few weeks about this and feel that God is directing me

elsewhere, but I don't know what that means. I have talked it over with my

father and wish that my mother were here to talk with. She always

understood the ways of God and my heart better than anyone."

My thoughts were racing, and my words tumbled out, "Luram, have you prayed about this? Is there another girl to whom Father is guiding you?"

"Not until last night. My father insisted that I pray, too. I did and had a dream, but I don't know if it is more than a dream. So, I thought we should talk. I can't think of anyone I would rather marry than you, but I want to follow God's divine direction for me."

"Luram, I, too, would be honored to be your bride but want only to follow God's wisdom. Tell me what was in your dream, and I will tell you of mine."

He looked both relieved and intrigued for I had said nothing about a dream until then.

"Alright, Lilly, but I have told no-one of these details, only of what I suspected it meant. I was in a mountain meadow, and you were there. Someone was standing behind the waterfall that I never saw—only the shadow. There was a voice from the forest calling to me to come back. It was a female voice, one I thought I recognized. Puzzled, I switch my gaze from you to the voice and then back to you. Another voice spake that only you could understand, but I could hear. You looked at me and encouraged me toward the other woman. Neither of us could see her, but I could hear her. As I turned, I saw you switch your focus to the waterfall, and I took a step away awakening with the sweetest feeling of joy. Lilly, what does it

mean?"

A tentative joy grew in his countenance as I shared my own matching

dream, in amazement and awe. God loved us both. We embraced but with

a new sense of future.

That evening, I told mother what had happened with Luram and how

identical our dreams were. She interrupted me, and we went to find father. A

first, he didn't look pleased. It was a good thing mother had spoken with him

before, but as I shared the remarkable details of both dreams and the mutua

feelings of joy, his countenance changed. He asked, "Lilly, how will you tell

Sam? Do you really know that he wants to marry you? I can't go negotiate

with his father, and I don't feel comfortable doing so with his mother; he is of

age now. What would you have me do?"

Over the following weeks, all that Sam had been hinting at and I

avoiding began to replay deliciously because now I was no longer hesitant. I

rapidly grew from admiring and liking Sam to loving and adoring this valiant,

gentle, manly man. He seemed to take the change in my attitude as if he ha

expected it. I don't know that he ever knew of my betrothal with Luram. I had

always avoided pairing-off with Luram during our activities even though our

fathers had "arranged" things. So, I suppose he just thought that Luram was

one of our group that I liked too. But now I felt free to see and compare without feeling disloyal. Sam was of a larger stature than Luram. But more

than that, his faith was obvious. He never hid behind popular opinion by

acting out what the group liked. He took initiative and was willing to lead,

though never seemed ambitious or proud. Sometimes, I felt like my size

made Luram seem smaller, but with Sam, it was as if we were made by God

to be together. I felt beautiful around Sam! I was filled with a sense of

belonging and security and… love!!

CHAPTER 4: An Impression See Alma 53 (64 BC)

"Sam, I love you so much and want to always be found by your side, but mother says our leaders are planning to join the Nephite army against the traitor, Amalakiah. Will you be going with them?"

"Lilly, how can they since none of us has any weapons and most have taken an oath to never fight again. It has been sixteen years since the great burial of our weapons, sixteen years without shedding blood. I can't help but wonder, has the addiction to taking another man's life been burned from their souls or will war rekindle that lust?"

"I don't know, Samy. I am afraid for my father and older brother. They are planning on asking all over the age of twenty-one to join our new army. But mother says that the Prophet Helaman is coming to talk to us on the Sabbath. Perhaps he can guide them to know God's will for us."

"Lilly, I have an idea that I need to check out with some of my friends. It may help all of us. I don't want to discuss it yet, but please pray for me. "

"Sam, what is it?" Then seeing the pleading expression on his face, Lilly said, "I am sorry. I will wait to know, but you will tell me as soon as you can, right?"

"Of course, Lilly, but you may not like it. Pray for me, for all of us."

I left Lilly to go find my friend Laman in his field. Once I shared my impression, He was excited. We decided to call our plan, '*stripling*'. We spread the word by dividing, each speaking with a different friend, dividing, and spreading until by evening we had begun something that would be heard by every teen in Melek by the Sabbath. Even my little brother Aaron was excited, but he was only twelve, so wasn't included in the plans

As usual, the day dawned sunny and hot. There was much excitement in the air for the Lord's prophet Helaman would be in our land today. We busied ourselves with our morning chores so we could be ready to join with the whole of our people to hear the prophet speak. Brother Ammon would be there too. We were his people as well as the Lord's.

"Sam, when are you going to share your plan with the elders?"

"I will wait for the right time, Aaron. I know that you want to be involved, but mother will need you to care for the fields. You will have more to do than any thirteen-year-old in the land. Be patient, God is certainly in this. It isn't my plan."

At that moment, mother's voice rang clearly, "Come children, follow your brother Sam. We must leave together now!"

The excitement of having prophet Helaman with us was almost more than we could stand. As we gathered with all the rest of our people, we found ourselves amid a great crowd. We hoped that we would be able to hear. The Elders sitting near where the prophet would stand seemed so small and far away. A hush seemed to pass through us all like a wave on the great sea.

We all stood, and I watched as Prophet Helaman passed to his place at the head of the gathering. To my surprise, as I looked about, I saw assembled to one side, an army of our fathers, brothers, uncles, and cousins. They stood at attention, armed, and uniformed. Lilly had been right about the plan to join the battle with the Nephites who had been protecting us for years. Though we had provided food, clothing, and weapons for them, I know some had yet felt guilty for not actually fighting.

I leaned over to Laman sitting near me and asked, did you know about this?

"No, not like what we see. I had heard from my older brother saying that he and father had been preparing for something. They had been talking about defending the family so that more would not have to die as did your father."

I was about to respond, when Joseph, our head elder stood and addressed Prophet Helaman, Brother Ammon, and the other great missionaries who had accompanied the prophet.

"Dear Brother Helaman, esteemed guests, and brethren, as you can see, we have decided as a people that we cannot sit idly while our brethren the Nephites are dying to both protect us and defend all the lands of the Nephites. We are now ready to lay aside our oath to our great God, Jesus, knowing that He will understand that our desires are righteous. I present to you our army of one thousand five hundred strong men who are now prepared to resume their training but this time as Nephite warriors with God to strengthen us."

I watched our visitors who at once became somewhat agitated except for the prophet. They began to confer with each other as Prophet Helaman rose and to my surprise he took Elder Joseph into his big arms and embraced him. He appeared to weep but it was difficult to tell from our distance. I glanced over to Laman who sat with mouth open. I looked to mother who was shaking her head from side to side. I heard the prophet speak, "Brother Joseph, how I love you for your desires and willingness to serve the Lord even at great sacrifice. You have undoubtedly wondered why your lives should be spared while your Nephite brethren give theirs to protect you when you are perfectly capable, even trained to protect your own families. I know that God is pleased with you and your offering, but you and these men of your assemblage, who were once great Lamanite warriors, have made an oath with Him. Our oaths, vows, and covenants are our way of demonstrating our faithfulness to God just as He demonstrates His faithfulness to us. To break your oath, even under this great national peril, is to say in your hearts that oaths are contingent on circumstance. Yes, God understands our logic even under the guise of self-sacrifice, but your heart will not. If you break your oath, you will always, from here on out, waver in your vows to God. Our sacred oaths and covenants cannot be at the mercy of circumstance. God's oaths are never broken, ever! Moses, the great prophet wrote that God declared, 'My word cannot return void, for as they go forth out of my mouth they must be fulfilled.' Likewise, we must grow so that our word is never void! Additionally, your people's oath has cost the lives of good men who have kept theirs even when self, family, and national defense could have served as a righteous excuse. But they knew that their lust for blood would again be kindled even in the defense of those they loved. They, therefore, submitted to the oath and God's mercy, and so have been cleansed by their faith in the Christ's great Atonement, a faith that came through their sacrifice, as it must be with us all, in similitude of that great sacrifice that will be made by the very Son of the Father. Joseph, my brother and all of you most willing brethren, please trust in God to show us another way than breaking your sacred oath!!

In that instant, I knew what I should do. I looked over to Laman, his expression told me that he, too, felt as I. We both stood—all eyes upon us. I spoke, but the words were not mine, "Prophet Helaman, sir", I called out loudly, "God has shown another way." I turned around and around, lifting my arms slowly into the air calling out, "Striplings, arise!" It seemed like time stood still as I turned and turned. Then almost as if practiced, some 2,000 teenagers stood silently, proudly, nodding their concurrence. A soft murmur spread across the assemblage as mothers and fathers spoke quietly and faithfully their assent as they offered their youth to God.

The prophet stood stunned. He turned to Joseph quizzically. Joseph whispered something to him, and he nodded. He called me forward. I took Laman with me, trembling, yet confident in God's direction. Once before the prophet, we bowed humbly. He seemed to wait for us to speak. He could see that some planning had already been started. "Sir," I began hesitantly, "We are young, too young to have made the oath of our parents. We are hard working and capable, though we have never fought. I followed an impression two days ago and started a message that passed quickly throughout our young men. We have called the plan, 'stripling' as you heard. We are indeed young and some of us are small, but we learn quickly and with some training and faith in our God, we will protect our families and our brethren the Nephites thereby allowing our fathers to keep the oath my father died to make. If our brethren, the Lamanites, would leave us in peace, we would never seek to fight, but there is a great need, now! Will you accept our offering?

The prophet smiled warmly; tears streamed onto his beard. "Are you the leader of this band of striplings?"

"No, sir," I stammered, "but if you, God's prophet, will lead us, He will give the miracle this nation needs. Our mothers have taught us to trust in Him and you. Will you lead and train us?"

He opened his arms to both Laman and I and drew us in. As he wept, he spoke, his deep resonant voice penetrating, "The Spirit whispers that I must, and I will captain these 'stripling warriors.' How are you called, young brother?"

"I am called, Sam, and this is my friend Laman, Sir."

"How old are you, Sam? Some of your friends may be small but you are large and formidable."

"I am eighteen, Sir, my father was a great warrior, but I have never fought…."

We quietly conversed like this for a few minutes before the prophet turned to the people saying, "I am deeply moved by your willingness to not only join the Nephite defense in such a time of need but more so by your willingness to offer your youth to such a cause, in the face of the dangers of war. All who can sustain these stripling warriors with me at their head, signify by your voice of assent." Suddenly there rose such a sound as I shall never forget. It was not a loud sound, yet it pierced our hearts and overwhelmed our senses as thousands of quiet parental voices united in a deep hushed thunder that swept across the gathering. Prophet, and now Capitan Helaman turned to the assembled army of fathers, brothers, uncles, and cousins and invited, "Men and brethren, the Lord accepts your willing offering—not to fight where the lust for blood would be rekindled but rather to now train these two thousand stripling sons to defend themselves and this nation. Will you accept?" Again, there arose a tumultuous sound—this time overwhelmingly loud in enthusiastic assent to the prophet's request. We were a united people in love, in faith, and in determination to preserve our liberty, home, family, and our rights to worship God, all which Amalakiah had sworn to abolish.

CHAPTER 5: Preparation

"Sam," said Lilly, "this means that you are going to leave; what if you don't come back; what if, like your father, you give your life?"

"I am sorry that I couldn't tell you, Lilly. I knew that this would upset you, but like your mother, your faith, your trust in our God, is strong enough to comfort you until we return. I don't know what His divine will is for us, but I trust Him."

"But what if He requires your lives to pay for all the murders committed by our people before their conversion?" bemoaned Lilly.

"No, Lilly, you have forgotten that when Christ comes, His atonement will pay for all of our sins, including those of all our converted people. Whether we live or die in this war has more to do with each of us individually, our faith, and His plan for our individual lives. Mother says that God will deliver us if we have faith, and I know the faith of my mother. I have seen it in our lives ever since Father surrendered his life. Look at your mother, Lilly, her faith is just as powerful. The story of the vision of her father is told in her very name! How can you doubt, my sweet lamb?"

"I know, Sam. It isn't that I doubt, I just miss you already! I will watch you train; perhaps they will let me train with you, so I can feel part of all this."

"You are strong, Lilly. I love you for your wanting to be part of my preparation. You will be a wonderful mother protecting our children."

"But Sam, you have not spoken to my father, we are not yet even betrothed, yet you speak of our children as if that is a certainty!"

"Lilly, I have waited and have been following a prompting to begin building our future home. I should be finished by the time we leave but had decided to wait to speak to him upon our return from this war. That way you will always know that you have a home."

"I am overwhelmed! Is that where you have been when insisting that you had duties to perform? So, Sam, if you are certain in your faith as you say, I would prefer being betrothed as yours before seeing you leave. Building the home confirms your expectation to return to my arms. I want to be yours and you mine for ever! Could you speak to him tonight?"

"Yea, I cannot say the smallest part which this makes me feel, Lilly. I feel your love, I love you too! Since you put it that way, and I cannot doubt that my mother also knows, I will talk to him this evening if he is willing."

A week later, early in the morning, found me standing with my 2,000 companions before Captain Helaman and our fathers and uncles, a betrothed man. The betrothal ceremony was warm and full of joy and tears. Lilly's father had been a great warrior and a man of great faith, a man of "the oath". He added to my faith and that of my mother that I would return. It seemed so strange to me, to now be holding a sword and shield. They felt foreign in my hands, but I knew that it was God's will. He had directed me in this, I knew for myself and didn't have to rely on my mother's faith. God had inspired me as a lad, as a fiancée, and now as a soldier in defense of God's people and kingdom on earth. There, before us, stood God's prophet holding Captain Moroni's title of liberty. It was now our standard, too!!

"In memory of our God, our religion, and freedom, and our peace, our wives, and our children"

I had read it many times before but reading "wives" this time brought a feeling and determination I had never felt before. The word, "children" filled me with a vision of the future that brought warmth and even excitement to my heart. I was going to help create my future. I was ready; I was determined; I was filled with the beautiful vision of my precious Lilly; my wife and mother of my children yet unborn! I was filled with a conviction of God's presence and power. This new feeling of strength and power seemed to well up inside as I imagined an enemy threatening my precious ones. I didn't know it at the time, but this warrior-mentality would help save our lives and make us divine instruments in helping save our country.

The training was to be short and intense for the need was immediate as Amalakiah had taken all the southern fortified cities. After some basic training, increasing our stamina, we began learning to hold the sword and then to thrust and turn, block, and cut. Javelin and cimeter training followed. thought that we would be trained with the bow and arrow, but, since we were all accomplished at hunting for food our leaders, we decided to focus on close encounter defense and offense. After several days of exhausting exercise, we were paired and caused to spar against each other. To my joy, I was paired with my friend Laman. At the signal he attacked with skill and confidence. I blocked his thrust easily but missed the use of his shield as he came around and clubbed me with it. We had not been trained in the offensive use of the shield, so I wasn't prepared. His father must have been working with him. I was much larger, so thought that I could easily defeat him, but as I shook off the shock of his strike, I realized that he was coming back around for another thrust. We were not to hurt each other but, he looked so very serious. I had been relaxed enjoying the mock battle but suddenly realized that if he were a Lamanite, I would be facing death. I quickly blocked the thrust and rolled to my side to avoid a new strike with his shield, but he was prepared and tripped me. I fell to my back with his sword at my throat and his foot on my chest. He smiled and laughed, but I did not. The next days found me far more intense in my conditioning and training. I asked Laman to teach me his additional moves and passed them on as we had done with the original message spreading it quickly to all.

Our departure-day was at hand, what we lacked in experience, we compensated in unity and faith. I loved these my companions. Even the smallest among us, maybe especially the smallest were amongst the most skilled—they knew that they had to be more diligent and seemed to have more divine assistance. We helped each other and worked through our individual needs. We protected and supported each other. With a prophet, who had trained with us, hurt with us, and prayed with us, we felt like mighty instruments of the Great Jehovah as we assembled for the last night's orientation with our families.

The big bonfire crackled as sparks ascended to join the myriad stars in the black canopy under which we assembled, not as companies but as families. To be surrounded and supported by those I loved whom I knew loved me, the very ones each of us had pledged to protect, united us like no words could explain. As I felt the close warmth of Lilly and the proximity of Mother, Aaron and my sisters, Lilly's mother, and father and family, I was consumed by the very Spirit that both weakened me and, as I had learned, filled me with strength and power like unto Nephi at the Bountiful shoreline before his conniving brothers.

Captain/Prophet Helaman spoke as did Brother Ammon. I don't remember their words, but I distinctly remember being overwhelmed with this uniting, empowering force that filled our hearts and muscles. I couldn't help but listen to the distant music of our river as it, too, praised God. I loved our home, I loved my mother, I loved my Lilly, I would protect my family! My attention was drawn back to our leader, "Are you ready, my sons, to follow me against the myriad of disciples of darkness; those trained assassins who would enslave your families and deprive them of all rights and freedoms?" There was again a resonant crescendoing cry of assent as we rose to our feet and thrust our stripling fists into the air. It took only moments for the thunder to die down as he spoke in reverent hushed tones. He bowed his head signaling our silence as he blessed us by the prophetic power of the sacred priesthood that we shared. The contrasts of mighty fierceness aside the reverent humility in our reliance on Jehovah set my head spinning with a mixture of excitement, awe, gratitude, and love. I had never been in this state before. What else lay before us??

Lilly had been watching me, "Are you alright, Sam?"

I could only nod and pull her closer to me, hoping that what I was feeling could be shared by closeness. Beneath the loving but watchful eyes of her father, she snuggled into my chest and whispered, "I miss you already, my noble warrior!"

CHAPTER 6: To Violence (See Alma 56) (64 BC)

Our military march to the city of Judea, where Prophet Helaman had been instructed to rescue the dwindling forces of General Antipus, was much different from our previous civilian march to Melek. We found that our conditioning really made a difference in improving the speed of our march and alleviating the fatigue we had fought against before. As we paused for a mid-day meal, Laman asked me, "Does this great valley seem smaller this time to you now than when we first entered?"

"Yes," I replied, "I was thinking the same thing. Why do you think that is?"

Laman paced, pondering and gazing around. He seemed to take in the high mountain tops shrouded in clouds, in the far in the distance. Then, as if a light dawned within him, he exclaimed, "It isn't that it looks smaller, but rather that we are able to march so much faster that it just seems that way, since we aren't lingering in chaos as before." Suddenly we heard the shofar trumpet the call to assemble. We quickly took our places in our company and were on our way again. Laman was right, we would be at Judea before tomorrow evening. Could Antipus and his men hold on until then?

Late the next afternoon, we became increasingly excited as Judea came into view across the wide plane on the other side of the River Sidon. However, as we entered through the battered gates opening to us, it was apparent that things had been exceedingly difficult. There were still bodies of the dead waiting for burial, men lying around in the shade with bloody bandages, and evidence of fire and destruction all around. I heard my friend Timothy whisper, "The Lamanites really do out number them, it is a good thing we are here." We were on a mission, and it was bigger than just the wicked Lamanites, it was the wickedness of the Lamanites. Conquering the enemy of all righteousness was imperative.

Prophet Helaman met with Antipus who couldn't stop rejoicing over our presence. I could sense his concern as he gazed upon our youthfulness. Our numbers were much appreciated, but untested in battle there was skepticism even amongst those whose wounds we began to care for. Prophet Helaman presented us as "my two thousand sons, my stripling warriors." We indeed felt like the sons of Helaman. He was our hero in whom we had great trust because of his closeness to Jehovah. He had brought us from boys to warriors, marched us across all the Nephite lands, led us in prayer and in the study of God's word. We felt like we were on a mission.

I heard Antipus explaining our now dire situation to several of the men including Prophet Helaman, "The Lamanite armies are exceedingly numerous. They have taken possession of all the cities on these southern borders, Manti…," he stopped and looked to those who stood up onto the wall pointing into the distance. We could see the smoke rising from the distant city of Manti to our left. His hand swept to the right across the plains along the foot of the great mountain chain. We could make out three other cities as he pointed: Zeezrom, Cumeni, and Antiparah. We didn't have enough warriors to even hope to recapture any one of them.

Our first assignment was to aid those left from the army of Antipus in strengthening our defenses. The Lamanites had come several times— surrounding the city and shooting fire tipped arrows into the bulwarks and support beams. They had tried to dig down the banks of earth and fill the trench leaving many weakened places to repair. Antipus' men were ragged, beaten, desperate, and far too worn out to shore up their only means of relative security. We went right to work with the cheerfulness of fresh, youthful muscles and music. Without meaning to, the spirit of the entire fortified city changed in one song with the voices of two thousand stripling workers unified in morale, strength, spirit, etc. As we worked, someone would start a song, and we would all join in spreading music throughout the city. When one song ended, someone would start another. Orders and directions seemed to fit between verses or were given by hand signs. Soon even Antipus' men were working alongside us with renewed energy.

"Sam, are you the one they call Sam," asked one of Antipus men.

"Yes, what is your name," I asked cheerfully humming while I lifted a large beam into place.

"I am called Captain Omner by my men. What makes your new men so different besides looking like Lamanites?"

"We are loyal Nephites, people of God, but our fathers were Lamanites before their conversion under the teaching of Brother Ammon and his missionaries."

"Ah, I have heard of your people, but I thought that you wouldn't take up arms ever again?"

"Yes, our fathers took that oath to keep their covenant of conversion. They feared less their addiction would rekindle the lust for killing again preventing true forgiveness, so they would rather die than take a life. They really did bury their weapons, and many gave their lives as a result. However, we were not of age and are not bound by the oath nor are addicted to shedding man's blood. God instructed us to join you in defending our country. Though we are young and untested in battle, we are strong and trust that if God sent us, God will empower us!"

"Sam, I must admit that before your arrival, we had all but lost hope. The few of us that were still praying see your arrival as divine intervention. We believe that you are indeed divine instruments. I must tell you that listening to you speak kindles hope and lights my faith! "

We passed many days in work, song, discussion, and testifying. We became aware that the Lamanites spies had taken note of our arrival with fresh supplies. The armies that held the four cities were becoming restless and began to prepare for the battle that they had postponed. Had they come before or after our arrival, it may have been fatal for this city. Judea and the city by the west sea were the only unfallen Nephite strongholds left. The evil Ammoron gave instructions for the Lamanites to stay and maintain the cities. We could not go against them, so there were several days of rising tension for fear they might secretly go around us to attack the weaker cities to the north.

"With the return of our spies, Antipus called our captains together along with Prophet Helaman to strategize against the Lamanite army plans. We would allow the Lamanite army to pass our city and fall on their rear the moment they met our armies defending the north in the front." But we were soon disappointed in our plans, for the Lamanites dared not leave their walled cities as Ammoron had commanded. What were we to do? How could we ever hope to recapture our southern border?

CHAPTER 7: Spies and Strategy

At that time of prayerful wondering about our overwhelming situation against so many walled cities, we were surprised by the arrival of provisions from our families. There is no way to express the joy we felt as we met the few that brought the food, clothing, sandals. We were about to divide all we received with Antipus men when the very next day an additional 2,000 men from Zarahemla arrived to assist in the recapture. The recruiting of additional warriors, we were told, was encouraged by our march past the city several months before. The Lord had found additional ways for our people to be a source of help instead of a burden.

The City of Judea now stood at 10,000 fighting men. The next day, I was called into Prophet Helaman's tent.

"Sam, I would like you and Laman to accompany two of Antipus' spies. We are concerned that the arrival of the Zarahemla brigade will excite the Lamanites to take action. We need to know what they are planning. You may not need to penetrate their defenses, but since you look like the Lamanites, you should be able to find additional options his spies won't have. Antipus has approved of this strategy but be careful and listen to the Spirit."

"Yes, Sir, Thank you for the opportunity. We won't disappoint you!" We turned and left only to meet the two men Antipus had sent: Josh and

Daniel. It took the rest of the day and much discussion before we trusted

each other sufficiently to enter such a dangerous assignment. We devised

hand-signals, so we could communicate from a distance. As we reached the

top of the last hill, before the city of Manti, we saw the Lamanite army

assembling outside the city gate.

"Josh, I am going to go down there before the Lamanites are finished

organizing and see if I can overhear their plans," whispered Sam

The enemy soldiers were still in disorganized confusion while I walked

from the trees to cross through the Lamanite camp as though I were going

somewhere specific. I just prayed that no one would recognize that I was a

new face in camp. The sounds of soldiers arguing surrounded me as I

advanced through the camp. It became obvious that some thought they

were to stay and hold the city while others argued they needed to stop our

resupply chain from strengthening us. An idea formed in my mind as I could

tell they were leaning towards leaving the security of their walled city. as I

was about to blend into the forest again and circle back around, I heard a

voice ask, "Where are you going soldier?"

I spun around, meeting the dark eyes of a very large Zoramite officer.

I was no small man either, though much younger, yet the Spirit filled me with

peace and the words to say. "I was looking for you, sir. We have been

ordered by King Ammoron to watch for any Nephite company leaving their stronghold and lie in wait to attack them, thus whittling down their forces, group by group."

"You stupid Lamanites, that is precisely what we Zoramite captains have been saying all morning long, but there is much dispute over King Ammoron's orders to preserve the city. This is good news, dismissed soldier." I waited until his back was turned before I melted quickly into the forest. I needed to report to Josh and Daniel immediately.

Our return to Judea to report to Antipus was hasty. Both Josh and Daniel felt that we had accomplished our mission as spies. Antipus was very pleased with the news and complimented both Laman and me on our willingness and follow-through. He ordered us to report to Prophet Helaman with directions to prepare our 2,000 striplings for a special decoy mission.

That evening, under Prophet Helaman's direction, we arranged our packs to look like they were full of supplies but left them light enough so that we could travel quickly in case of need. We were apparently going to march toward a city down by the sea but pass close to the Lamanite strong hold of Antiparah.

"Sam, you were involved in this decision to have us march to the sea. Why do you suppose that we are being sent as a decoy rather than going as trained warriors? Is Antipus afraid that we are too young and inexperienced to trust us with a real assignment?" asked Jacob, another of our younger striplings.

"Jacob, I wasn't really part of the decision, only the informant. But from what I saw, all the Lamanites need is an excuse to leave their walled city and we are going to give it to them. They, too, will think that we are an easy target as a young supply convoy. Once out of their city, Antipus will attack and fight. Who knows, we may end up fighting as well, but we must trust God in this."

Afterwards, I could see Jacob periodically talking to others that would gather round him during the rest of the evening. We were to leave at first light, so I wanted to get a full night's sleep. As I was about to extinguish the torch, Prophet Helaman called at my tent door.

"Father Helaman, I am honored and surprised. How can I be of service to you, sir?"

"Sam, thank you for your respect. But I am just like you, my son. I am honored to be called your father. I truly do have 2,000 sons that I love dearly. That is why I have called on you tonight. The others look to you as a leader, they confide in you their fears and concerns. Tomorrow, we will take all precautions to avoid direct fighting though I have confidence in our preparations, I also have concerns for our inexperience and tenderness of your youth and purity. To expose you to more atrocities and bloodshed seems unjust. But please, can you share with me the morale of our stripling warriors?"

"Thank you, Father. I know that we are all very anxious for tomorrow. Some look forward to testing their battle skills against God's enemy. Others may be frightened but they bury their fear in faith. For most of us, He is the God of our mothers, since most of us hardly knew our fathers. It is natural to think of our mothers when we think of faith. Besides, we love that we are led by God's holy prophet!"

We embraced as he whispered a choked "thank you" before leaving. Like so many others, even though the light was put out, sleep did not come easily as we re-lived our training skirmishes in the dreams of the night. Tomorrow was upon us!

It didn't take much to gather the troops for food and assemblage. Most of us carried rather than ate our morning meal—we were just too anxious to serve our God. We had spent so much time speaking of war and preparing for combat that when the time had arrived, we felt…the shofar sounded. Action replaced our thoughts, and we left the security of the walled city. Not only were we in the open, but we were to march within an arrow shot of Antiparah. I was especially conscious of the agitated Lamanite mentality. To see us was to attack us! We were 2,000 strong, but they were seasoned, ferocious warriors who numbered several times that. It would take us most of the day to come near their stronghold and timing was critical. Antipus was to follow us at a distance and remain unseen by the Lamanite spies.

The only sound we heard was the sound of our footfall, two thousand in unison, as we pondered our upcoming encounter. We had had a special prayer before we left where the prophet had pronounced a blessing by the power of the holy priesthood upon us. Some immediately but reverently shared their feelings with those around me. As I listened, I realized we all shared a powerful sensation like we were mounting on eagle's wings, soaring with God. Something sacred was happening to us because of this priesthood blessing, our faith, and diligent preparation! I was again overwhelmed.

The city walls came into view, and we could see the sentries pointing in the far distant. We picked up our pace and gave the appearance of fear as we passed on our way to the city by the sea. Having been informed by their spies, they were waiting to march after us. Their city gates opened, and they began to flow forth as like locust swarming over ripe grain. We began the rapid marching we had practiced. We counted on being in better condition than the Lamanite army. We had marched like this for whole days. We also knew that our passing near to Antiparah would signal Antipus' departure from Judea, but the Lamanites' focus on eliminating us kept them unaware of another army yet hours away. The rattle of our swords and spears combined with the rapid footfall gave an eery sound to our march. The roar of the war cry came from the massive army behind us—now in full pursuit. This was designed to fill us with additional fear, but instead I caught a glimpse of Laman, he was smiling. Our plan was working.

We march-ran the rest of the day. We had no problem keeping the distance between us. By late afternoon, we were a considerable distance from Antiparah. Antipus should soon have access to the city. Suddenly, a warning cry came from our rear guard. The Lamanites were speeding up and would be upon us before Antipus could come to our rescue. We were 2,000 soldiers against the innumerable horde of Lamanites and Zoramites. One of our lookouts reported that they had seen Antipus marching from their rear and thus had sped up without turning to the right or to the left supposedly hoping to destroy us and turn to finish off Antipus. We sped up to match the Lamanite speed hoping that Antipus would be able to match them. We continued like that the rest of the daylight. As night fell it was evident that both the Lamanites and Antipus had made camp. We knew them to be exhausted because we could feel the effects of our daylong run. But how long would they sleep knowing that they would be surrounded if either Antipus or our army turned or caught them during the night? We slept on our swords that night if we slept at all. Prayers and devotionals were heard throughout the camp until silence finally descended.

At first light, the sentries sounded the alarm so that all our training to rise and march with haste paid us in the peace only known to the prepared who trust in God. We again marched all that day leading them away from their stronghold and into the wilderness. They were afraid to turn lest we Nephites should surround them, so we all marched with haste until it again turned day to night.

"Sam," bemoaned Laman, "How long can they keep this up. I thought that our conditioning would outlast them long ago, but they keep coming!"

"I, too, expected this to go differently as well, but we must trust in God who knows all and will work things for our best. I hope and pray for Antipus and his men who haven't had the rapid-long march training as we have—having been couped up within the walls of the city or fighting for their lives, all these many months. Come, we must rest; I have a feeling the Lamanites are desperate enough to march in the dark if they only knew the lay of the wilderness. You can count on them moving before first light anyway!"

The night felt so short when, suddenly, we could hear the charge of the Lamanites at our rear. They must have come over the rise to find us bedded down at the base of the hill. Fortunately for us, there was a deep ravine they had to cross first. Prophet Helaman had the foresight to have us cross it even in the waning light as the sun set. Now it stood between us and the horde. We were up and out of camp even faster than the morning before.

To our surprise, they had halted, probably at the ravine or just over the hill. Were they hoping to decoy us into turning and falling into their snare, or had Antipus come to their rear in fear for our safety?

Prophet Helaman called us to council. It was the third day of our march and of the seventh month. In hindsight, I see this as providential, for our forefathers in the old country knew this month as the strong month, the completion of creation month. This was to be the completion of our plan and the beginning of God's work in regaining this part of our land. The prophet Helaman restated our dangerous situation and the possibilities before us, Behold, we know not but they have halted for the purpose that we should come against them, that they might catch us in their snare; therefore, what say you, my sons, will you go against them to battle?"

There was but a momentary silence as we looked into each other's youthful faces. We had trained for this moment without desiring it. But the thought of Antipus fighting that horde, without our support, churned within me and apparently in others. The prophet looked to me first supposing that I could represent our united feelings. While looking around again for assent, I said in a voice loud enough for most to hear, "Father, behold our God is with us, and he will not suffer that we should fall; let us go forth; we would not slay our brethren if they would let us alone; therefore, let us go, lest they should overpower the army of Antipus."

Instantly, all heads nodded in ascent, swords were raised, and a reverent murmur swept the striplings. In awe that we should feel so reverent in a moment of such great danger, I continued, "We came to protect the liberty of our fathers, our mothers, and our families. We would sooner give our lives for their liberty than live to see them enslaved! When many of our fathers gave their lives for their oath, our mothers began to teach us the value of the oath, the value of life, the value of liberty whereby the great God of our Fathers can lead us to a fullness that will allow us to return and live in His presence together. All through these years our mothers have not only talked of this but also lived it in great faith. They have performed miracles with that faith, so there is no doubt that our mothers knew it! Our mothers have taught us that if we would not doubt, God would deliver us!

Father Helaman bowed his head, remained quietly in reverent awe. When he looked at me again, he peered through water filled eyes, and smiled—too overcome to speak. He motioned to me to assemble the stripling sons; we were off to the first real battle of our lives.

CHAPTER 8: The Test of Reality

After crossing through the ravine and climbing the hill, our eyes swept the awful scene below and in front of us. Everyone we could see were moving away from us as we watched in horror our Nephite brethren fighting but without direction, all was in great confusion. "What is happening?" I asked no one in particular. The deep voice of Father Helaman offered an explanation, "Perhaps Antipus and his leaders have been slain or wounded already, leaving their men in confusion. Certainly, the rapid march has exhausted all but especially those that had to shoulder command. Come, my sons, it is time! They are about to fall into the hands of this enemy. Go with God, sound the attack."

To the sound of the shofar we came upon their rear and began to slay them with astonishing force. I, myself, was surprised at how each powerful blow of the sword or cimeter seemed to instantly take the life of a vicious enemy preventing the slaughter of another of Antipus' men. Our two thousand had such an overwhelming effect that the entire disorganized, blood-thirsty horde halted their pursuit and seemed to turn upon us. The thunder of their blood-cry designed to frighten us, filled us with gratitude — gratitude that the lives of Antipus' men would be spared. We later learned that Antipus' men, even without command leadership, upon hearing the blood-cry and seeing the change in Lamanite direction and focus, united as if led by invisible forces to fight anew. They recounted that they rose, filled with concern for their "young brethren" and crashed into the rear of the Lamanites with renewed and massive power, slaying all in their path.

Though fully engaged against a skilled Zoramite captain, my gaze was momentarily distracted from my fight as I caught a glimpse, over my enemy's shoulder of Laman falling wounded at the hand of a huge Lamanite warrior. In my distraction I felt the tip of the enemy's sword slash my arm, I was bleeding but that brought me back in full force as I saw him raise his sword for what he hoped would be the death blow. Remembering the very move that Laman had taught me, I parried his blade, ducked under, and ran my sword through my worthy opponent. I could take no time to reflect upon his life and future as I quickly came to Laman's aid as the giant was thrusting downward again and again at the rolling Laman. With a mighty blow from behind, I also sent him to stand before his God.

Though it seemed like we fought all day, the sun had no sooner reached its peak than the Lamanites were compelled to deliver up themselves as our prisoners along with their weapons of war. Father Helaman would later tell us that he observed the fear of the Lamanites as they saw that we could fight with a miraculous strength greater than any they had ever encountered. Unable to resist our attacks and blindsided by our strength, they delivered themselves up fearing for their lives.

My immediate concern, following the surrender, was upon the welfare of my stripling brothers. Father Helaman arrived at that instant of my thought and command us to assemble, so he could number us. This was a brilliant way to resolve those concerns that had grown since rescuing Laman. I knew that I couldn't be there to rescue all of them but hoped that they had come to each other's aid. So, as they slowly took their assigned place in the company, I counted anxiously, wondering over who would be missing. To our great joy, not one place in the assemblage was empty. None had fallen— though each stood bleeding. Father Helaman looked heavenward with great awe and as his gaze descended, he saw and heard four thousand knees bend to earth to thank the Lord of Hosts. None had doubted, none had faltered, even while being struck, slit, pierced, and wounded. Though we were the sons of Father Helaman, we knew we were the sons of God, and He had chosen to protect our mortal lives. Thus were our thoughts as we marched back to the city of Judea while our prisoners were taken to Zarahemla by the survivors of Antipus. Little could we know, in our jubilation, that our real test was still months away.

CHAPTER 9: Aaron See Alma 57 (63 BC)

With the death of Antipus and the largest army of the Lamanite's southern front now captured, Father Helaman wasn't surprised to receive a letter from the evil Lamanite king, Ammoron. It had been almost five months since our initial but unsuccessful campaign to recapture Antiparah. Though the Lamanite army had been decidedly vanquished, we too were suffering. We needed to return to Judea, now closer to us than Antiparah since we had fled northward. There we could heal our wounds and regain strength from so many months of battle.

"Sam," Father Helaman approached me as soon as we had arrived back in Judea and after he had read the message, "What do you think of this offer to trade Lamanite prisoners for the whole of Antiparah? You have been to the city."

I was momentarily taken aback that the prophet was asking for my opinion. "Sir, I can't see that there are enough soldiers left to defend the city after God has given us this victory, and we have sent their survivors to Zarahemla. It seems like Ammoron is up to his usual schemes wanting something for nothing. Surely, we can take the city now without exchanging prisoners!"

"Thank you, Sam. Those are precisely my thoughts as well. I will offer to exchange their prisoners for ours; that would only be fair though Ammoron hasn't been known to fight with any honor."

As we settled in to make repairs and heal from the last battle, days seemed to run together until some months had passed. Ammoron eventually refused our offer, so we began to prepare to go against the city of Antiparah before it could be reenforced.

"Sam, are the warriors ready to march to Antiparah?"

"Yes, sir, but there has been one of our spies sighted approaching the city! I think that we should await his arrival before beginning our march."

The spy was none other than my beloved friend, Laman. He had healed from his wounds and served valiantly. He entered the city with great speed and came directly to Father Helaman's tent, without having received word from us.

We embraced. "Laman, greetings, my friend! Do you come from Antiparah?"

Father Helaman stepped from his tent to join our conversation. "Yes, Sam. Greetings, Father Helaman! I bring news of Antiparah. This morning the gates opened, and all the remaining people left to join the other southern Lamanite cities. The city is ours. Our other spies entered and secured the gates. Praise God, for he has given us this victory without additional bloodshed."

"Or loss of prisoners!" Father Helaman remarked as he looked towards me. I smiled and explained to Laman Ammoron's offer to exchange prisoners in return for the city. "This is glorious ending to this twenty-eighth year of the reign of the Judges," he rejoiced as Laman, and I happily nodded our agreement. It had been almost a year since we first planned for this and almost two since our departure from home.

While we celebrated a new year with prayer and song; we were surprised when one of the lookouts sounded the shofar! I was immediately dispatched to the top of the wall. I could see a large force of men approaching Judea, but unexpectedly from the north, a direction that wasn't Lamanite...I was confused until I saw their Nephite banner. It was a much prayed for supply and reinforcement company. We descended to receive them, and I could only feel overwhelmed with gratitude. Father Helaman joined us as we swung open the gates, took charge of the supplies, and assigned the six-thousand warriors their quarters. I was filled with such happiness at God's goodness when I heard a familiar voice call my name as the warriors passed towards their assigned corner of the city. I had been so preoccupied with delegating all that was necessary to care for supplies and living arrangements that I had not noticed that in addition to those six-thousand Nephite warriors were sixty of our Ammonite brethren who had grown up, prepared, and qualified to join in the defense of our country and rights to worship. I didn't know who had called me. I scanned the sixty until my eyes landed in disbelief on my little brother, Aaron. I lunged forward and tried to sweep him into my arms, but it had been almost two years since we had seen each other, and it was a time of growth and maturity. He was no longer my little brother! His arms wrapped around me as we both tumbled to the ground laughing and rejoicing together.

We stood, slapping each other with brotherly joy. Aaron reached inside his pack and handed me several small, folded papers. "What is this, Aaron?" I asked.

"These are secret communications from a certain beauty who prays mightily for your safety. It is no wonder that you are still alive!" He said, half seriously. I was filled with a feeling that I hadn't experienced in a long time. I had sent a few communications back with supply requests but didn't know if she ever got them. I had often lain awake at night talking quietly to her in the darkness. After two years, the chance to read her thoughts captured my total attention. Father Helaman's deep voice brought me out of my reverie as he addressed the new arrivals. I wanted desperately to disappear into some quiet place and read her thoughts.

As most of our soldiers were finishing securing the city and my immediate duties were all completed, I settled in a private place and removed the folded papers from my pouch. Each was numbered and dated.

There were ten in total—each written approximately a month or more apart.

The first was written just days after our departure so long ago.

Sam, my beloved,

You have been gone for several days now, but it seems like a lifetime. I fondly remember your silhouette in the moonlight. I miss your laugh, your soft and tender touch, the gleam in your eye!!! Since our separation, I love you a thousand-fold more. I have tried each day to see you and imagine what you would be doing, but I fail and begin crying. It is difficult to continue without you, but God is sustaining me. I feel His merciful hand. As I begin to long for you, He fills me with His love, His peace, and acknowledgement of the sacrifice we are both making. Somehow, He understands, and I feel it deep within my soul. I pray for you each day and night and often during my daily tasks. I walk by your home each day or so experiencing the memories and warmth of our time together. Those memories inspire me. You have always influenced me for the better.

Aaron and I reminisce about you and your great bravery and faith. He nearly worships you! I pray that God will protect you and fortify you!

Now that you and all the other warriors are gone, the village seems so empty. Receiving visits from other families, who share our same concerns, is a tender mercy from God. As we visit about our shared heartache, we have decided to gather each week after worship to pray mightily together for all

the warriors and conclude our fast. Fasting helps us care for our poor and

allows us to feel that we are contributing to your mighty force. Never

misjudge or deny my most faithful heart. Ever thine, my dearest Sam.

I will write again,

Lilly

Warmth from Lilly's letter permeated my heart. But part of me wanted

it to completely fill that empty place I had come to ignore. The other part

wanted to race and read each of the other nine, but I wanted this to last. It

was as though reading each letter would be like binging Lilly here with me. I

would savor this moment and have yet more over the next several days. I

drifted off to sleep with sweet memories of my Lilly.

CHAPTER 10: The Cumeni Miracle (Alma 57–63 BC)

I woke with a start. Apparently, my mind had been mulling over a troubling thought through the early hours. Why was it easier to have faith in God for my own safety but another thing to trust that my not so little brother, Aaron, would be safe in battle? I looked over, in the morning twilight, to see his sleeping form curled on his mat. My prayer that morning was a bit longer as I counseled with the Lord over that concern. I knew that God had protected and empowered my 2,000 brothers, but I also knew that each of them had a powerful faith in God and were prepared to die for our families and country. Was I weak for the anxiety I felt concerning Aaron's safety? I had spent my life protecting and mentoring him. Now he was a man, and though not as large as I, I had seen over the last several days that he was proving to be a skilled warrior. In counseling with God, a question came into my mind, "Do you trust me with his life and wellbeing?" I pondered that for a moment realizing that I knew that whatever happened to him would be the wisest thing for his life, like it was for mine. I could trust, but I had to replay the question and the sweet feeling of love that accompanied the thought to stop worrying every time I started to plan our next efforts to regain our lost cities.

After Father Helaman had refused King Ammoron's belligerence and Antiparah fell into our hands, secured with part of our army, the next logical move was to take back the city of Cumeni. If only they would come out to battle against us. But with their cities reinforced and their largest army defeated, they remained secure behind their fortifications. A council was called together with Father Helaman in command.

"Men, the Lamanites will not leave the protection of their fortifications to battle us. Cumeni is protected with the very strong walls constructed under Captain Moroni's instruction before the Lamanites took possession. How can we recapture this city?"

A large Nephite officer by the name of Zoram spoke first, "I could only see two possible approaches which I took to the Lord: One, we have enough men. We could surround and battle them, working to dig down their ramparts. Or two, we could again lure them out with a small force and do as before, surround and defeat them. I have not received any clear answer, so I put it before the council."

An older Nephite, with white hair but a strong hardened body, stood animated but calm, "It is good that you have been praying Zoram. But I feel that you have not received an answer because neither option is advisable. The Lamanites tried to dig down the ramparts of the fortified city of Noah about the time that the people of Ammon were moving to join us. Those Lamanites were all killed as they tried, and so the city stood. I was there! Option two worked because it hadn't been done before. The Lamanites know that we are numerous and strong. They will not leave their stronghold without

compelling enticement."

All in the counsel nodded their agreement, even Father Helaman

seemed to see the wisdom and experience of this wizened old warrior. He

spoke, "Listening to your good thoughts and ideas has sparked something."

He went on to share his ideas and we all felt the Lord's approval. We were to

surround the city with our considerable army to lay siege effectively cutting

off their access to more supplies so they would eventually come out against

us. If we are divinely guided, we might even intercept their resupply forces.

Leaving a large contingent to guard both Antiparah and Judea, the

remainder of our forces marched toward Cumeni arriving just before a

resupply caravan. We established our defenses and surrounded the city.

That night we slept on our swords ready, at any moment, to go into battle as

we had desired. The Lamanites attempted to secretly attack in small groups

but our guards were alert and Lamanite blood was spilled. Several days

passed and we knew they were getting worried when by night the supply

caravan attempted to enter the city right through our Ammonite section of the

siege. Thinking that we were a Lamanite escort, stationed for their

protection, they entered amongst us and we easily captured them without

bloodshed. We knew that they greatly needed supplies. As predicted, they

began by sending out small groups to steal food, but our guards caught them each time. Seeing that the supplies might be lost in battle, we sent them, with a small force, to Judea and the growing contingency of prisoners to Zarahemla.

One morning, after several days of starvation, a small group of Lamanite soldiers surrendered to our guards, on condition that they might speak with our leader. Father Helaman summoned me, and we went together to speak with the prisoners. He explained that he wanted my help in case they tried to deceive us. But they had simply lost all hope of any help coming from Ammoron, and therefore wanted to secure food for their soldiers offering their complete surrender. Unlike the Lamanites, we cared for our prisoners as if they were our own soldiers, and they knew they would be fed. That night we took complete possession of Cumeni.

Our great success in obtaining the city transformed into a problem. Our numerous forces, with which we knew we could conquer our enemy, were now forced to guard that enemy.

"Aaron, how did it go on guard duty last night?" I asked.

"It was terrible and even dangerous. We were faced with either killing them or letting them escape. They found clubs and stones to attack us. There is a burial group working for their dead. I don't know how long this can last; we have already put two thousand to death."

"Thank you, Aaron, I must agree. I had better counsel with our officers. I feel that we need to do something differently than slowly slaughtering them as they try to escape. Some of our own men are being hurt by them. It is natural for them to want to escape, so we must change our plan. Perhaps we should send them all to Zarahemla."

After our counsel and approval by Father Hellman, we did just that. A portion of our men were selected to guard the prisoners all the way to Zarahemla under command of Gid. He left that afternoon. But to our surprise, the next morning, a large Lamanite army, sent by Ammoron, came upon us. The battle was fierce!

"Aaron," I yelled as I blocked and twisted to avoid the blade of a Lamanite Cimeter, "behind you!" But I was too late, or Aaron didn't hear. I watched in horror as he was cut down by two huge Lamanite warriors. "No," I mourned, and finished off my opponent with a fake, a dive, and a roll followed by a chop from behind to his helmet, ending my immediate confrontation. I ran, praying, towards where I had seen Aaron fall. The two warriors were moving to verify his demise when I dispatched one from the side and engaged the other. We battled far too long, I needed to check on Aaron. This giant of a Lamanite was not used to being matched, but he did not have the strengthening hand of God. Fear began to fill his eyes as I slashed, turned, parried, rolled, and cut—finally dislodging his sword and knocking him to the ground unconscious. I didn't take time to see if he was gone. I knew that if Aaron was still alive, he would need immediate assistance. As I felt for his heartbeat, I heard him moan. He was alive! He slowly regained consciousness, and I became aware of the battle around us. Our army was falling before the superior enemy force. Suddenly, I heard a battle cry, it was ours! Over the hill came Gid and his warriors that we had sent with the prisoners. I would later learn that when the prisoners had heard the cries of our spies returning with the news that the Lamanite reinforcements were attacking Cumeni, they had run in one body onto the swords of Gid's forces. He slew most, and the rest escaped, so he had marched with speed to assist in saving us. With their arrival and the incredible strength and skill of our little band of 2,060, we prevailed until the Lamanites took flight back to Manti.

Father Helaman had fought side by side with our little band. His commands were brilliant, even inspired, and we obeyed him with exactness. As the Lamanites fled, he turned to me and said, "Sam, take several of our sons and search among the fallen for the wounded. Hurry, they will need saving." I told him of Aaron—now under care; I knew he would be well after giving him a blessing. I hurried off to do as he commanded me. We found about two hundred of our striplings who had been wounded but not slain.

As we left to search that day with ten or so of my brethren, the sun bore down on us making us more conscious of the suffering that someone unconscious or unable to move would be feeling. The hills were strewn with the bodies of the dead. Some of our soldiers were beginning to dig graves. It was a gruesome sight and even more gut-wrenching to stop and check each one for signs of life. Fortunately, we were only searching for our striplings. To our surprise we weren't finding any until….

"Aaron, look by that large boulder, is that Laman?"

We commenced running, with Aaron arriving first. "Sam, it is Laman, but he is still alive!" We quickly began washing and anointing his wounds with water and olive oil. We erected a small shade from the cut branches of a tree. As we worked, he began to stir.

"Laman, your wounds don't look as serious as we first thought. How are you feeling?"

"Ohhhh, Sam, the last thing I remember is hearing something behind me while I was fighting a large Lamanite. The next thing I knew, all was black."

"You must have been struck from behind and left for dead. Your faith has preserved you! They normally would have run you through or taken your scalp to make certain you were dead."

This scene was repeated over and over as we all scanned through the bodies. By the end of the day, we had either dragged or carried about two hundred of our striplings to camp. After we returned with the first ones, others joined us in the search while the burial detail continued to work around us. As the number of striplings continued to enlarge at the camp, the men began to marvel. Not one stripling was found dead. Each had received many wounds, but none were dead! Father Helaman rejoiced with us as did the whole army.

They had fought with the strength of God, remembering the words of their mothers to never doubt but have faith in God who would preserve them. It was a miracle, considering the reality that we had lost a thousand of our Nephite warriors to this battle but not one of our striplings. Though we gave it no heed, the whole of the Nephite army credited our victory to Gid's return and the faith and skill of our little band of striplings. Faith is an interesting force that allows anyone, even in the face of impossible odds, to trust the wisdom and power of an unseen God, sufficient strength to step into danger, knowing that either God will empower you or take you home. But these two thousand sixty had been promised deliverance by their mother's faith, and so trusted God's prophet to lead them to victory—death was not in their considerations. The repetition of this miracle first with our two-thousand and again with the additional sixty bore witness to our entire army of the strength of the Lord. This had to be more than youthful vitality, special skill, or

coincidence. They knew it and it increased their care and diligence in their

daily devotion to God. We led by example, and all were blessed by it!

CHAPTER 11: Manti (Alma 58 – 63 BC)

It was late into the next day when I was summoned to Father Helaman's tent.

"Welcome, Sam, how are my wounded sons fairing this afternoon? It is such a miracle that not a single one was killed!

"Thank you for asking, Father Helaman. They are doing well; most are ready for battle again. We are continually humbled by the miracles we see in their stories, both of the preservation of their lives and in the speed of their healing. Laman should be dead by all accounts of his last fight and his wounds. I am yet amazed that they didn't take his scalp as they have with other casualties. That would have ended his chances for recovery. We are also grateful that the Lamanites fled from the city."

"Indeed, my son, Cumeni was a great victory but only a third step along a series of cites that have been occupied by the Lamanite armies on our Southern border. Since they also abandon Zeezrom, they have all fled to Manti. We will do well to maintain the four southern cities we have. Unfortunately, since they have gathered in Manti, their army far exceeds ours in number. By this time, we seem to have exhausted all our strategies, so that the Lamanites are cautious and will not allow us to lure them from the safety of the walled strongholds. Sam, if you are certain that you have tried everything you can think of to decoy them into the open, I think that we should wait for them to send us reinforcements from Zarahemla; what do you think?"

"Frankly, I am surprised that we haven't received additional warriors already, Father. Perhaps something has gone wrong in Zarahemla?"

"That is a sobering thought. Much can happen during war. I will send an embassy to governor Pahoran to inform him of our desperate situation. With the increased enemy numbers, it may be that they will begin to counter-attack and even capture any reinforcements and supplies. We really need another ten thousand warriors if we are to survive much longer. For that matter, we desperately need food. That embassy must leave immediately!"

During the next several months, the Lamanites did come against us but only in skirmishes retreating quickly to their stronghold. We were unable to effectively engage them, and none of our own efforts, to capture their supply guards or reinforcements, were successful. Our situation was becoming critical. Finally, when we were prepared to send another embassy for help, a guard of two thousand warriors with a food supply made it through enemy attacks. Perceiving such meager help, Father Helaman began sharing his concerns for the spiritual welfare of our nation. One evening, after our war council had met and discussed the state of our army and plans for harassing the Lamanites, his tone turned very sober.

"Brethren, I am filled with a sense of foreboding, as if there is something worse happening within our government. We must call the men to a day of fasting and prayer. As we weaken, the Lamanite forces seem to strengthen. If we are to retain our cities and our lives, we must have divine assistance. Do any of you have any counsel for us?"

A solemnity distilled over us. No one spoke but all head nodded in understanding and agreement. We concluded to fast together in two days time. The next days passed in a flurry of Lamanite attacks, repair work on the city wall, traveling to check on the welfare of the other cities, and much prayer. Father Helaman called us together to teach us from a copy of some portions of the records he had brought with him. The stories from our fathers were most strengthening to our faith. We knew we could trust God. The day after our fast and final prayer gathering, I woke with a strange sense of peace that persisted as I gathered with others for our morning meal. As we talked together, it became evident that we had all awakened with the same sense of assurance for deliverance. Personally, I realized that my life had been a series of experiences where a great feeling of helplessness was followed by deliverance. My faith, in God's deliverance, in all circumstances, was greatly strengthened. Father Helaman taught us of the coming Son of The Father who would come to deliver us from both death and sin. To hope for resurrection and eternal sanctification seemed like a continuum of our mortal lives. He truly was the Deliverer. That morning as we met with an already elevated mood, Father Helaman spoke to us again.

"Men and my sons, thank you for your fasting and prayers. We all have experienced that some things don't come out save by fasting and prayer. I have felt to re-read Captain Moroni's Title again. Though our forces are relatively small and our food dwindling, we must remember that we fight for a cause that is just. Here, let me read, 'In memory of our God, our religion, and freedom, and our peace, our wives, and our children.' How would you feel if you were to enter your home and find the enemy threatening your family, your wife, or your little ones? I know your faithfulness to God and His commandments. I know your trust in His empowering force. I know that you would rise in His strength and might to save those you love. We know what the Lamanites would do to our rights of worship, our nation, and our homes. Could we ever surrender to be slaves? No! We must conquer with God at our side!"

In unison, we rose to our feet. In unison we cried, "In memory of our God, our religion, and freedom, and our peace, our wives, and our children." We had all learned to pray with that on our lips. We believed our cause; we felt the power rise within us! Somehow, we would endure through this crisis and conquer with God as our ally! That very day we gathered behind Father Helaman with all our might to go against the teaming city of Manti.

"Sam, instruct the whole army to pitch their tents on the wilderness side of the city."

"Yes, Father, that will give us room to fight or flee!" instructed our warriors to arrange our camp so that we spread out to look more numerous than we were. But when the Lamanite spies came out the next morning, they could easily see that they well outnumbered us. Yet, since we were by the wilderness side, they feared that we could block their supplies from coming in. This proved both advantageous and dangerous. We had tried for months, without success, to find a way to lure them out from their stronghold, and now they were preparing to come out to battle. They feared our position but not our numbers which was the dangerous part. This is where a prophet leader becomes essential. Father Helaman called to captains Gid and Teomner, and me to come immediately to his tent.

As we entered, He was kneeling next to a small map of the city and our camp that he had drawn on the dirt. He looked up and motioned us to him.

"Gid, I would like you to take a third of our warriors and secret yourselves here on the right of the road in the wilderness," he pointed on the map, "Teomner, take another third of our men to this position on the left of the road and secret yourselves from the passing Lamanite army on the road." Both men looked curiously to the prophet wondering what he intended. We were already outnumbered, so to divide us into thirds seemed

dangerous. But his prophetic mind had received a plan that combined all the

strategies of our previous victories into one the Lamanites would not

suspect. "Sam, I will join you as we occupy the empty tents of our whole

army to make it appear as if we are waiting for their supply convoy. They wil

come out, thinking that their numbers will make it easy for them to eliminate

us, which they easily could do even if we weren't divided. Once they are out

of the protection of the city walls and about to fall upon us, we will rapidly

retreat into the wilderness with hopes they will follow us. We know what to

do, as we did with Antiparah. We must stay ahead of them, leading them

from their stronghold. There will be spies and city guards left behind, but Gic

and Teomner should be able to overpower them once we and their main

army are deep into the wilderness."

As we retreated deeper into the wilderness towards Zarahemla,

Father Helaman called me forward.

"Sam, it won't take them long to realize that we are heading towards

Zarahemla. I hope that our government still has control of the city, so the

Lamanites will fear coming too close. I am feeling that they will stop their

pursuit and camp for the night as is their custom. I want you to send spies

back to signal us when they camp, so we can pass by them in the night bac to Manti. They will suppose that we too are weary and that we are the whole of our army."

"Yes, Father, surely God has inspired you. We can take the longer route back to Manti, avoid them completely, and still arrive in Manti before they can get there tomorrow!" As I called Aaron and Laman to me with instructions, I marveled at the wisdom of God in placing a prophet at our head.

From Manti's walls, we watched as the Lamanites came wearily through the trees into the clearing around the city. They were obviously disappointed they hadn't engaged us but certainly relieved to have chased us from their supply road. As they returned to the city gate and found it shut, they expressed dismay. We could hear them from our hidden vantage point above them on the wall.

"Commander, the gates are closed and seem blocked! Surely those lazy guards we left behind are sleeping in fear that the Nephite swine will capture them. How do you want us to proceed?"

Taking advantage of their disorientation, I signaled our warriors to rise and fire a volley of arrows below. The astonishment and sudden danger to their lives filled them with such fear that they fled in chaos from that quarter of the land, taking only a few slaves with them as a token of victory back to Ammoron. We suppose that their superstitions will leave them wondering at the Nephite miracle that gave us control of their strongest city in the region. But how to maintain those four cities we had recaptured was the new problem. With the Lamanites gone and our troops guarding the cities, families began returning as we strategized and prayed for safety. Surely, if the Lord had given us victory so many times, He would protect us as we awaited our government to send more help though Father Helaman expressed concern that there might be some faction in the government inhibiting them.

CHAPTER 12: Home (Alma 59-62 – 62-57 BC)

It was some years later before rumors began circling the cities that the war was over. We anxiously waited until we received an epistle from Captain Moroni declaring the end of war…, Ammoron had been slain in the northeast, and the Lamanites chased back into their lands in the highlands to the south, save a certain number who, as prisoners, had come to know about the gospel and joined the rest of our families back in the land of Melek. Finally, Father Helaman called us all together to disband our army. We assembled one morning with much anticipation amongst us.

"Faithful Nephite Warriors and my stripling Sons, I greet you in the name of The Lord. It is in great praise and thanksgiving that I now release you to return to your homes and families. We must note that God has delivered us, and, in a miraculous way, shown us the power that comes when faith is combined with exact obedience by wondrously preserving every single life of our two thousand sixty stripling ammonite warriors."

There was much show of approval and rejoicing as the entire army celebrated together. Among our striplings, there was much reverent embracing for a few moments until we were overcome with gratitude for our merciful God. When little Aaron, who was now big Aaron, tearfully released me from his now muscled arms, I fell upon my knees, overwhelmed. Strangely, all two thousand sixty followed as if struck in that instance with humble gratitude to our Father for this miracle. This seemed to stun the rest

of the Nephite warriors, and their jubilation and reverie was quickly replaced

by a reverent hush, and they too fell prostrate. Father Helaman then

expressed the feelings of our hearts to our unseen God in ways that perhaps

only prophets can. The reverence lasted for a long time as we slowly rose

embracing each other. Can Warriors in battledress love each other? We

certainly were filled with that love as we packed and disbanded over the next

few days.

Our march back to Melek was filled with anticipation mixed with

memories of our seven years away from our loved ones. Oh, my loved one,

Lilly, I am coming! We passed through the great valley but then detouring

over to Zarahemla as instructed by Father Helaman. As we descended

towards the city, I was struck with its beauty, the river, and the mountains in

the distance. I wished for a painting, so I could gaze upon it every day.

As we marched at the head of our striplings, Father Helaman spoke, "I

never tire of this view of our capital. God has blessed us with a beautiful land

and the liberty to enjoy it. Sam, I know that you haven't seen this big city

before. I want to establish a camp on this side of the River Sidon. We will

rest here and resupply, then I will turn the striplings over to you to take them

home to Melek. I want to show you our city and introduce you to some of the

leaders. It is likely that Capitan Moroni and Chief Governor Pahoran are here now. You have been the hand of God in helping save this land. I want them to meet you! I want you to meet my beloved and my family too."

"Father Helaman, I am honored and would rejoice in meeting them all, especially your family. I have heard so many stories of Capitan Moroni, and of course, learned and lived by the 'Title of Liberty'. I don't know if I can find words to say, I am only a boy!"

"No, Sam, you may have been a boy seven years ago when God inspired you to gather the striplings. He seems to prefer beginning with boys and girls and turning them into mighty instruments in His hands. You have become one of those, my son. You will one day lead your people, a holy people!"

I was stunned by his assurances and vowed to listen to that still voice that had been leading me these many years—that voice with which I watched my mother lead my fatherless family so many years before. "I will do as you say, Father!"

The next days were memorable. I was overwhelmed to stand in the government palace and meet Chief Judge Pahoran. He was a mighty man beginning to age though, as indicated by his snow-white hair. He had faced such a harrowing time with the Kingmen-coup, yet now commanded respect and obedience. His presence was immediately felt as he entered the chamber, yet when I was presented to him, he rose, embraced, and thanked me. I could not speak. But my awe was even more boundless when I stood in the presence of Captain Moroni. I expected a commanding presence with a steel gaze that would stop a leopard in its tracks. But instead, I met a mighty, humble man who deferred all my praise to God, who had forged him. He was even more my hero ever after.

Shortly thereafter, Father Helaman took me to his home. I didn't even know what to expect. As we neared, there were people gathering to celebrate his return. He laughed, saying they were like family. He lived near the edge of the great city, along the river. I could look across and see our large camp in the distance with the striplings mingling about. I knew they were anxious to return to their families but needed to rest and recover from wounds and battle fatigue. We finally arrived at the path leading to a modest but most beautiful home nestled in the trees on the edge of fields and vineyards. His family came out in response to the rising sound of the crowd. That was the first time I saw Father Helaman as the father he really was. His Anna was elegantly beautiful. Several small families that I later discovered were his children and grandchildren surrounded them. They mobbed him with their affection; He was a happy grandfather. I stayed for dinner that evening but knew that I had to get back to my companions. Dinner was simple, and I basked in the love felt in the family unity I longed for with Lilly— just a few more days!!

We gathered at the garden entrance after dinner. All present could sense my desire to be headed home. I looked into deeply into Father Helaman's eyes as I took his hand. "Goodbye, Father Helaman. You indeed are the father I lost as a boy. Thank you for trusting me and teaching me! Your example will ever be my light as I follow our Savior!" We embraced; tears ran like the Sidon itself. I quickly returned to my companion warriors preparing to break camp with the first light of morning. We were going home!!!

CHAPTER 13: Blissful Love (60 – 57 BC)

From a distance I could barely see the walls of Melek through the trees. The mountain backdrop and our own little river formed the perfect picture of paradise that had been in my dreams for seven long years. We marched ahead not knowing what and who would we find. Written news had all but ceased over the span of fighting and the dangers for a lone runner with the Lamanites so close. Our last real detailed news had come with our sixty companions five years previous. Some of the Nephite reinforcements had brought rumors but little satisfying detail. I had sent letters each time prisoners or emissaries were sent northward. Had they ever reached Melek? I had images and dreams playing continually in my mental theater. But there before me was the reality. It looked so much like my imagination that I was certain my family would still look as I left them even though my mind tried to correct the notion so as not to be disappointed.

As we approached, singing together a song of victory and faith—sounding like giant curloms crashing through the forest—the village gates opened! Though we were still at some distance, we could see people slowly, curiously coming out to investigate. As if in unison, they all began to jump, hug, and celebrate. We learned later that a runner had notified them that we would be coming in the next days. Soon we were close enough to recognize faces, each of us searching then pointing as we continued singing. Elder

Joseph stood in front right next to Mamma. I ran, she shuffled into an embrace that could have lasted the rest of the day. I love you, Mamma. I can hardly wait to tell you of God's hand in bringing us home…into your arms, I whispered into her ear. And, then I saw her standing in the shadows behind Mamma! My mouth went dry, and nothing came out as I continued to mouth the words of thanksgiving. Aaron noticed the change, looked to see what I was staring at He nudged me, laughing. It didn't take long for the rest to follow leaving our songs of praise to transform into laughter, names, and expressions of joy! Though I led these stripling warriors, all I could think of was sweeping her into my arms. I released Mamma as she too noticed the change in my attention, then closing the distance all too slowly….

"Oh Lilly, my beautiful, darling betrothed," we spun around in a magnificent embrace.

"Sam, my brave and handsome warrior! I have missed you more than there are words to describe! My prayers have been answered! I love you so! Thank our God for your safe return."

Saying anything to the rest of the striplings would have to wait. Our dismissal seemed to happen as we returned to our families and hoped-for-families. What would the next days without guard duty, fighting, planning, scheming, be like? After seven years, I didn't even know how to imagine it. Suddenly, there was the sound of the shofar, the village Elder stood high upon his speaking stand. A surprised silence settled over the whole of us even though all we really wanted to do was hold and talk!

"My people," called Joseph, now bent with age. "We have counted the days when we would finally be able to honor these young men for their sacrifices. Sam, are you the commander of this powerful force?"

"Elder Joseph, I have served as the liaison for Prophet Helaman. We are excited and honored to be home. Thank you for your public consideration. I know that it has been a sacrifice for all of you as well. I am certain that there will be many stories told over the next few days as families are reunited. It is my privilege to report to you all, that God has been merciful to us, not only in giving us victory, but in preserving our lives. Seven years ago, we departed with two thousand stripling warriors under the Prophet's command. You sent us sixty additional warriors along with food for which we were most grateful. We have returned with two thousand sixty men with faith in God as strong as steel!"

I was about to continue but was abruptly interrupted with a cheer from the villagers that were still assembling. I thought of our dismissal assembly that ended in all of us falling to our knees in gratitude for our lives and anticipation for our homes. And here we were! As the thunderous mix of voices and clapping continued, I stepped away from Elder Joseph with an embrace and turned to find Lilly. She stood demurely to one side. I was overwhelmed with feelings of love and gratitude for her. She had endured such a lonely wait for seven long years. We had much to catch up on. We found Laman, our friend, now chaperone, and slipped away as people continued celebrating.

"Lilly, the moon light makes your hair glisten! I have missed you so much and fear that I will be awkward with you. You are so...so...beautiful, unlike any of the striplings. I have spent years with those who focused on battle, fighting, and hurrying. You are so...did I say beautiful? So refined... so pure and clean. Your very presence speaks peace and home. Lilly, I..."

"Please stop, my warrior, my Samy. I am nothing if I am not yours. I am what I am because of you. I have dreamed of this moment for so many years, sometimes I thought it was all a dream I made up. What we are, contains not only who we have been but what we will be. That will come as we build together. You had battle plans; we need to make strategic plans too. We will take things slowly and carefully. I already feel safe in your presence, I will feel even more in your arms. We will soon be married, but I know that unity is love, and love is a gift from the Holy One. You have been His instrument and will continue to be so as the father of our children. You have commanded warriors. Now you will mentor sons and protect daughters. I love you, Sam, more than life itself!"

"Lilly...I was...uh, I am...uh, I will be, but now I am just jelly with my tongue bound by boyish awkwardness. We will be married; I have pondered that reality every day and every evening. It lulled me into the far reaches of celestial visions by night, and delicious imaginations by day. But..."

"Shhhh...I love you, Sam. Stop talking, we are now home, our home, it awaits only our forever marriage. When will that be, my love?"

The next day, despite my desires to only be with Lilly, I spent time with Mamma. She was slowing down and needed help with her home and garden. As I worked, we talked,

"Mother, how I have missed your presence, though your faith never left me. How can I ever sufficiently express my love and gratitude for you and father?"

"Oh, Sam, you are so endearing! I am grateful to call you my son, but we should be talking about your wedding day. It has certainly been a sufficiently long betrothal! I have already spoken with Joseph who will officiate. He suggested that we could be prepared by the end of the week since you already built your home before leaving. Why did you do that without even being betrothed?"

"Oh, Mother, you taught me to follow those impressions with exactness. Now am I not so grateful? I can not stand another moment without Lilly! How did you know you could talk to Elder Jospeh without making certain all would be well with us?"

"You are not the only one with impressions, my son. I spoke with him the moment we received news the war was over, and you were coming! It will be a delightful day and wedding night under Abrahams's stars. You don't know it, but Lilly has already prepared her wedding dress, and your sisters have helped me with the food. Though with two thousand fifty-nine guests I am not certain we could ever be totally prepared. Now don't worry, go prepare your home, though you will find that Lilly has used those seven years to do much already, with my permission, of course."

The next few days past faster than a single day in battle. It was filled with preparations, I ended up retelling battle stories to the young who were oblivious that we were preparing for eternity. Also, there were always chores and to-dos from my precious Lilly. We worked to make our house, our home even though the village leaders were rumored to be planning something for me. Lilli, Aaron, and I stayed up late with our two families sharing some of the miracles of divine intervention. They couldn't get enough, and we were filled again with such joy at the telling.

The day finally arrived, and mother was right, there was really no way to prepare for so many guests. All my fellow warriors came accompanied by their families. I think the whole of Melek came bringing their own food and drink just to continue the joy of celebration over our return. If they came for no other reason, when Lilly removed her veil to seal our covenant with a kiss, her beauty would have been sufficient. I felt that my eternity began that very sacred night!

After our honeymoon together in Zarahemla where I took her to meet Father Helaman and Sister Anna, visit the temple, and show her the city, it wasn't hard to keep busy. I also missed Aaron and the striplings. I longed for Sabbath days where we could see everyone at worship, and I could renew my covenant with Jehovah. I longed to get the ugliness of war behind me, and the fighting dreams replaced with peace. Lilly was patient with me as I would awaken either calling orders or crying out warning. The worst was waking up standing in bed swinging my arms as if in battle. She was gentle though she too sometimes had to avoid my imaginary dream battles. We talked things out, remembering, when I could talk about it. God had blessed us with life, though each scar told a story. She wanted to know them all, but sometimes I couldn't relive it. Though we went in the strength of the Lord, which she loved to hear, each story usually ended in death for those who we should have been able to call brother if not for wicked leaders. Occasionally, one of our former prisoners would come by to meet my family as a brother, rather than as the enemy we had known before their conversion in our prison camps. I loved those times as we testified together of the mercies of a just God.

Life continued, day in and day out until one day Lilly arranged a special meal for us. We were alone again, and the food was most savory. As she served, course after course, I began to wonder over what would cause such a feast. As I finished the last dish, well satisfied, if not a bit uncomfortable, ready to sweep her into my arms in gratitude, she sat and took both my hands, locking eyes with me. They were a soft brown that gleamed in the firelight. She smiled and quietly spoke words; I could not grasp for meaning. "Sam, you are going to be a father." What could she mean? I did hope someday to be a father, but what did that have to do with this sumptuous feast? She just waited, smiling; her lids lowered as she looked at her belly. Light invaded my questioning stupor! As my face finally showed understanding, I swept her into my arms, standing and dancing with her around and around. "When?" I asked excitedly.

The discomfort of childbearing seemed to linger on and on…"next fall" seemed like years away. I was swept by the village elders into the village council. Meetings and assignments helped the time to pass for me but for Lilly the time seemed to slow each week. Spring came and added to the work of cultivating our fields and planting our garden. Even though she grew uncomfortably larger, she worked every bit as hard as we shared the load.

Along with our field of grain, I had obtained several animals that furnished eggs, milk, and some cattle to raise and sell. God prospered us, but our focus seemed to be on the coming of the newest member of our household. Almost every day, Lilly wanted to review her growing lists of possible names: one for boys and one for girls. The thoughts of raising a little human and helping them love the Lord and share eternal values gradually replaced my war dreams. I had learned faith from Mamma and exact obedience from Father Helaman. I wondered at times, how he was doing. I knew that he was out preaching and managing the affairs of the church. In some ways, I wanted to be with him to continue fighting the real war against evil at it roots. But I had my own roots to cultivate here as our "next fall" was becoming "any day now." Would it be Lilian or Samuel?

Aaron, my warrior brother married in time to become, to us, big Aaron as little Samuel was born. I didn't know how to hold so much joy. His bride was perfect for him, and little Samuel looked like the perfect mix of Lilly and me. Husky and big but strikingly handsome with his mother's thick dark hair. What adventures await him and how can we help him without interfering with his own agency filled my thoughts. We pray for guidance as we begin this, our own parental adventure. We will need much guidance!!

CHAPTER 14: A Zion City See Helaman 3 (46 BC)

The days transformed into years as news came of Moroni's retirement, followed three years later by Father Helaman's passing. He had worked to re-establish the church after so much evil and war. Our Ammonite settlement grew and prospered as did our growing family. The legendary faith of the striplings continued to unite our growing city as righteousness and prosperity spread through the whole land of Zarahemla. As we all prospered, many went northward by large ships to colonize those unknown lands. There were other things transpiring as well that didn't bode well for the Nephites. Over the ten years following our return from battle, I was given more and more responsibility over the affairs of our growing city.

As I write this from the lands northward, I clearly remember the awful contention that began around Zarahemla. It came with the death of two of the sons of Governor Pahoran in succession, at the hands of a secret society that rose when his third son was denied leadership. It didn't help that a dissenter left Zarahemla and was given command of a Lamanite army who returned to slay Pahoran's second son having succeeded his first son as the Governor. As the leading Elder of our city, I determined that if we were to continue building our Zion, we would need to move northward to separate from the growing Nephite and Lamanite contention.

In time, our move northward was so reminiscent of our move to Jershon so many years before, only on a much larger scale. Some of our people had gone ahead a few years before, so we anticipated finding some established dwelling place where we could continue our traditions and practice our religion. After we passed through a narrow neck of land, we noticed that the land was most fertile except for the absence of trees. What destruction had cleared this land of desolation? I later learned that there had been a people called the Jaredites who had self-destructed in this land. We passed through much of the growing settlements formed when others, years before had come northward. With only wood they could obtain from shipping they had mostly constructed their cities from what they called cement. We took care to learn how to make and mix it, so we could likewise establish our city while waiting for trees to grow. Hopefully our brethren would already have something for us, we didn't know how far northward we needed to go.

We have succeeded in establishing a Zion city, with a holy people of "peaceable followers of Christ." My family now numbers thirty with little grandchildren growing and learning the ways of happiness. Our first born, Samuel is part of our church leadership, I am so proud of him and his little family. He continues to study the records and preach with amazing clarity. My brother Aaron is raising a beautiful family not far from us. We gather at every sacred, holy day to sacrifice and dine together. My best friend Laman went with a group of families even further into the north countries. We have not seen them for several years now. Rumors come to us from time to time, of the increasing contention in the lands southward, which saddens us but makes us grateful that Jehovah has led us away from it all. We often receive righteous pilgrims from both Lamanite and Nephite societies. They love the Lord and could not continue to raise their families in such secret combination driven societies. Surely, the Lord has purpose in establishing us far enough away yet close enough that we could serve such wonderful families. We long for Him to come as prophesied. He lives, I have seen Him.

CHAPTER 15: Samuel See Helaman 13 (6 BC)

I remember as Samuel grew, we did our best to help him know and love the

Lord, who we both knew and loved. One day, I was watching him play with a

neighbor child who had come with his mother to visit. The child fell and

began to cry. Little Samuel, even at his young age, chattered something that

seemed to sooth the child as Samuel had come to hold him. Where had he

learned that?? Certainly, he had been treated that way by us but never had

we coached him in compassion at an age when survival, competition, and

self-interest, seem to dominate development. I watched as the two cheered

up and went back to their play. As a teen, that natural care for others

seemed to sweetly ripen. He loved to play sports, anything with a ball, and

he was very coordinated, so he excelled but never lost his compassion for

his teammates or even the opposing team. Often, he could easily have

scored but would pass off the ball so a teammate could score and would

then join in the circle of congratulations to heroize that teammate with no

thought about what praise he could have had. Who taught him that?? I was

so proud of him and loved him even when he made mistakes in judgement or

bad choices. I marveled at how he would learn from those mistakes,

apologize, make-up for any damage and move on, a better person. Once,

as his interests began to include the young women, who before had only

seemed like competitors, he was found alone with one of the leadership council member's daughters. They said that they were just talking but to find them alone at their age raised concern that spilled into public knowledge. Instead of becoming defensive for their lack of judgement, he apologized to her father in one of the council meetings and then publicly in a sabbath gathering. The two remained friends but nothing romantic ever followed, so it was all forgotten.

In the next few years, he focused his life on serving, as well as studying the sacred records. I began to worry that he had been so hurt by the earlier accusation that he was over compensating by not being close with any young woman. Fortunately, Lilly and I had become close friends with a family that we loved very much. Their daughter, Sariah was a beautiful girl with a strong testimony of Jehovah, preparing herself for the coming of Christ. She was just a couple of years younger than Samuel, so after much parental conferencing, we arranged the betrothal. Samuel was not only compliant but thrilled with our prayerful choice.

We watched the years pass as Samuel and Sariah raised a sweet family. Samuel accepted many calls to serve in the church, first as teacher and eventually as a leader. But strangely, his attention was always drawn to those Nephites who migrated to us from the south. They always brought news of growing secret combinations and wickedness. We felt so much gratitude that we had separated from them so many years ago that, now in the twilight of our lives, Lilly and I could know such peace. But Samuel was nearly obsessed with how the Nephite nation could be saved before the nearing coming of Christ, who we anxiously awaited. To him, their self-destructive course only needed one more prophetic voice to sustain the prophet Nephi and bring change. My correspondence with the Prophet signaled his own growing concern over the state of affairs in the land of Zarahemla, so after much counsel with the city leaders and the elders of the church, Samuel volunteered to go southward. The dangers he would face were sufficient to bring us in fasting and prayer to know if we should support him in his desires. If he went, his mother and I might be saying good-bye in our dwindling mortal state. Lilly and Sariah clung to each other as we all waited for divine guidance, hoping to stop him from going and potentially leaving Sariah to finish raising the children alone. The waiting only increased Samuels press to go. He had already received his answer and knew God was in it...he felt called to preach, warn, and more if required. It was after many days, on a Sabbath, that I woke to the clear impression, almost a vision...I could perceive in the eyes of my mind, my spiritual mind, Samuel standing on the wall of Zarahemla with stones and arrows flying all around him!!! What was I to make of that. Should I tell anyone or just share the peace that I felt as I watched in amazement that he could not be hit. I shared that peace with Lilly and went to sit with Samuel. He greeted me warmly and I could see that he was already prepared to leave.

Father, thank you for coming, I know that it is getting more difficult for you to get around. I was hoping we could have a talk before I leave. God has revealed to me so many things that the Nephites will want to know, or at least some of them. God has made it known to me and perhaps to the prophet Nephi, that Christ, our Messiah will be born in our past land of Jerusalem as Nephi saw…in just five years. We will be blessed to know it by a marvelous sign of a day a night and a day without darkness, perhaps because of a new star that will appear in the heavens!"

Samuel, are you certain, five years!! Oh, my son, your mother and I may even live to see that, what I gift that would be!! "

Yes, Father, and it will be preceded by many heavenly signs to help bring people to believe and repent. But I am afraid that it may even polarize the people! The rest of what I have been given includes the signs of His death many years later. Yes, as King Benjamin taught, He will suffer more than any man can suffer. The earth will mourn, as well, resulting in many changes in our land. There will be storms, winds, lightening, thundering, earthquakes that will leave all solid rocks in cracks and seams and more. There will even be three days of thick darkness before He comes to our people. But then, oh, that glorious coming!!! I cannot utter it! Please, share this with mother, I must leave, at once!! They must know!! I pray they will

listen, for their lives and posterity depend on it! Goodbye my beloved fathe

I wanted to tell him what I had seen…that God would protect him…but he

was off in such haste, having already gathered his family around him and

prayerfully blessed them, held them and said goodbye. Perhaps he already

knew?!

THE END

ADDENDUM 1: <u>Mormon and Moroni: What Happened to the People of Ammon?</u>[5]

"Having established an outpost that far north, the people of Ammon may have prompted other migrations to the land northward that occurred at the time. Mormon records that "an exceedingly great many…departed out of the land of Zarahemla and went forth unto the land northward to inherit the land…. Therefore, a group of perhaps over twenty thousand people migrated northward. (See Alma 63:4; Helaman 3:3-4)

It is a good assumption that the father of Mormon, a righteous man, had left the land of Zarahemla, fleeing to a safe and spiritual location. This could easily have placed him in the spiritual Mecca of that time…where Mormon would have been tutored in the priesthood and observed by his teacher, Ammaron….

Those who had migrated—perhaps the people of Ammon who had moved north… —are, in fact, the only real candidates for the 'peaceable followers of Christ' whom Mormon taught 'in the synagogue which they had built for the place of worship' Moroni 7:1-3).

In summary, the people who had a 'peaceable walk with the children of men' in the days of Mormon and Moroni (Moroni 7:4) were neither

_____

[5] The lives and travels of Mormon and Moroni by Jerry Ainsworth; chapter 14; PeaceMakers Publishing, ©2000

Nephites nor Lamanites in the traditional sense. Throughout the Nephite-Lamanite nation, 'wickedness did prevail upon the face of the whole land' (Mormon 1:13). 'There were no gifts from the Lord, and the Holy Ghost did not come upon any, because of their wickedness and unbelief.' (Mormon 1:14) From Mormon's childhood until the destruction of the Nephites, all Nephites and Lamanites who were in the land of Mormon's jurisdiction lived in a state of spiritual and moral degradation. Other (Nephites and Ammonites) had migrated to distant lands northward. Mormon states the converts of Ammon "never did fall away." (Alma 23:6-7)

ADDENDUM 2: STRIPLINGS IN AUTHORITY QUOTES
Joy D. Jones

Primary General President in Conference April 2017 "A Sin-Resistant Generation"

"The Spirit will inspire us in the most effective ways we can spiritually inoculate our children.

To begin, having a vision of the importance of this responsibility is essential. We must understand our—and their—divine identity and purpose before we can help our children see who they are and why they are here....

Second, understanding the doctrine of repentance is essential for becoming resistant to sin. Being sin-resistant doesn't mean being sinless, but it does imply being continually repentant, vigilant, and valiant....As James said, 'Resist the devil, and he will flee from you.' The stripling warriors 'were exceedingly valiant for courage … ; but behold, this was not all—they were … true at all times in whatsoever thing they were entrusted. Yea, … they had been taught to keep the commandments of God and to walk uprightly before him....'

Our children don spiritual armor as they establish patterns of personal daily discipleship. Perhaps we underestimate the abilities of children to grasp the concept of daily discipleship. President Henry B. Eyring counseled us to 'start early and be steady.' So a third key to helping children become sin-resistant is to begin at very early ages to lovingly infuse them with basic gospel doctrines and principles—from the scriptures, the Articles of Faith, the For the Strength of Youth booklet, Primary songs, hymns, and our own personal testimonies—that will lead children to the Savior."

Elder Jorge M. Alvarado

In Conference April 2019 "After the Trial of Our Faith"

"The influence we have on our children is more powerful as they see us walking faithfully on the covenant path. The Book of Mormon prophet Jacob is an example of such righteousness. His son Enos wrote of the impact of his father's teachings…

The mothers of the stripling warriors lived the gospel, and their children were filled with conviction. Their leader reported:

"They had been taught by their mothers, that if they did not doubt, God would deliver them.

'And they rehearsed unto me the words of their mothers, saying: We do not doubt our mothers knew it.'

Enos and the stripling warriors were strengthened by the faith of their parents, which helped them meet their own trials of faith."

President Henry B. Eyring

In Conference October 2016, "That He May Be Strong Also"

"We all are aware of the fiery darts of the enemy of righteousness being sent like a terrible wind against the young priesthood holders we love so much. To us, they seem like the stripling warriors, who called themselves the sons of Helaman. They can survive, as those young warriors did, if they keep themselves safe, as King Benjamin urged them to do.

The sons of Helaman did not doubt. They fought bravely and came off conquerors because they believed the words of their mothers. We understand the power of the faith of a loving mother. Mothers provide that great support to their sons today. We holders of the priesthood can and must add to that support with our determination to answer the charge that as we are converted, we are to reach down to strengthen our brethren."

Elder Jeffery R. Holland

In Conference October 2019, "The Message, The Meaning, and The Multitude

"When a child reads the Book of Mormon for the first time and is enamored with Abinadi's courage or the march of 2,000 stripling warriors, we can gently add that Jesus is the omnipresent central figure in this marvelous chronicle, standing like a colossus over virtually every page of it and providing the link to all of the other faith-promoting figures in it."

President M. Russell Ballard

In Conference Oct 2002, "The Greatest Generation of Missionaries"

"In one of the most powerful and instructive stories from the Book of Mormon, the people of Ammon had covenanted never again to take up weapons for the shedding of blood. But 'when they saw the danger, and the many afflictions … which the Nephites bore for them, they were moved with compassion and were desirous to take up arms in the defense of their country' (Alma 53:13). Helaman and his brethren persuaded them to honor their covenant with the Lord.

The scriptural account doesn't tell us who first pointed out that their sons had not made the same covenant their parents had made. I like to think that it was one of the young men who suggested the possibility that he and his peers be allowed to 'take up arms, and [call] themselves Nephites.'

'And they entered into a covenant to fight for the liberty of the Nephites, yea, to protect the land unto the laying down of their lives' (Alma 53:16–17).

This was an extraordinary task for a group of 2,000 young men, but they were extraordinary young men. According to the scriptural record: "They were exceedingly valiant for courage, and also for strength and activity; but behold, this was not all—they were men who were true at all times in whatsoever thing they were entrusted.

'Yea, they were men of truth and soberness, for they had been taught to keep the commandments of God and to walk uprightly before him' (Alma 53:20–21).

The rest of the story tells how these young men fought valiantly against the much older and much more experienced Lamanite army. According to their leader, Helaman, 'They ... fought as if with the strength of God; ... and with such mighty power did they fall upon the Lamanites, that they did frighten them; and for this cause did the Lamanites deliver themselves up as prisoners of war' (Alma 56:56).

While we are profoundly grateful for the many members of the Church who are doing great things in the battle for truth and right, I must honestly tell you it still is not enough. We need much more help. And so, as the people of Ammon looked to their sons for reinforcement in the war against the Lamanites, we look to you, my young brethren of the Aaronic Priesthood. We need you. Like Helaman's 2,000 stripling warriors, you also are the spirit sons of God, and you too can be endowed with power to build up and defend His kingdom. We need you to make sacred covenants, just as they did. We need you to be meticulously obedient and faithful, just as they were.

What we need now is the greatest generation of missionaries in the history of the Church. We need worthy, qualified, spiritually energized missionaries who, like Helaman's 2,000 stripling warriors, are 'exceedingly valiant for courage, and also for strength and activity' and who are 'true at all times in whatsoever thing they [are] entrusted' (Alma 53:20)."

President Ezra Taft Benson

In April 1986 General Conference,

"You have been born at this time for a sacred and glorious purpose. It is not by chance that you have been reserved to come to earth in this last dispensation of the fulness of times. Your birth at this particular time was foreordained in the eternities.

You are to be the royal army of the Lord in the last days....

"In the spiritual battles you are waging, I see you as today's sons of Helaman.

Remember well the Book of Mormon account of Helaman's two thousand stripling

warriors".

Sherri Dew of The Relief Society General Presidency

In BYU Speeches, 3/21/2000 "Living on the Lord's Side of the Line," excerpts

"There is such safety on the Lord's side of the line, where the power of the priesthood and the Holy Ghost protect us.

So how do we stay on the Lord's side of the line? How do we stand in holy places and be not moved? There is a great deal we can learn from Helaman and his 2,000 stripling warriors.... These young men were ultimately victorious against a larger, more experienced Lamanite army for several reasons:

1. Before the sons of Helaman began their campaign, they entered into a **covenant** 'that they never would give up their liberty, but they would fight in all cases to protect the Nephites and themselves from bondage' (Alma 53:17). It is the same with us. **The first step toward consecration and total commitment to the Lord is making covenants with Him.**

There is *power* in making covenants.... Having the Holy Ghost with us—and learning to hear His voice—is ...the single most profound key, to remaining steadfast and immovable on the Lord's side of the line. And it all begins by making a covenant.

2. The 2,000 stripling warriors not only made covenants, **they kept them**. 'They were men who were true at all times in whatsoever thing they were entrusted' (Alma 53:20). Very simply, they did what they said they would do. They weren't always looking for ways to straddle the line between right and wrong.

The stripling warriors not only kept their covenants, but they performed 'every word of command with exactness" (Alma 57:21). In other words, they kept their covenants with precision. A half-hearted effort to keep the Sabbath day holy or be morally clean or tell the truth or dress modestly is really no effort at all…. lest we lose control of our thoughts, our motives, or our actions and step into Lucifer's territory where we come under his control.

Living as Latter-day Saints is not easy. But it is easier than the alternative. The cost of discipleship, as high as it may be, is less than the price of sin—less costly than having the Holy Ghost withdraw or losing self-respect or jeopardizing eternal life.

3. The stripling warriors **were believers**. Their faith in Christ was active and dynamic. They believed that He could move mountains—not to mention battalions of bloodthirsty Lamanites bent on their destruction—if they had faith in Him. Thus, when asked to put their lives on the line, they responded without hesitation, 'Our God is with us, and he will not suffer that we should fall; [so] let us go forth.' They believed that 'if they did not doubt, God would deliver them' (Alma 56:46–47).

There is a reason that faith is the first principle of the gospel, because it is our willingness to believe Christ, to believe that He will do what He has said He will do, that activates the power of the Atonement in our lives….

No doubt most of us here believe the Lord can do these things. But do we believe that He *will?* They 'fought as if with the strength of God; yea, never were men known to have fought with such miraculous strength; and with such mighty power' (Alma 56:56)…. Every one of these young men was wounded, and at one point they nearly starved to death (see Alma 57:25,

58:7). Yet instead of wavering, they turned to the Lord and pled for strength—which they received (see Alma 58:10–12). Having faith didn't make their challenges disappear.

4. The stripling warriors' **faith began at home**, where 'they had been taught by their mothers, that if they did not doubt, God would deliver them' (Alma 56:47).... The lesson for us is clear: Choose carefully who you listen to, and then listen.

5. **Happiness and lasting joy come only from living the gospel.** Said Helaman after leading his 2,000 into battle, 'I was filled with exceeding joy because of the goodness of God in preserving us' (Alma 57:36). Joy and righteousness are inseparably connected....

There are many other lessons we could learn from the sons of Helaman. We could talk of service and selflessness, of obedience and consecration and endurance. But I turn now to the final and, perhaps for our purposes here today, most compelling point.

6. In this account in the book of Alma, it was **the rising generation who bolstered and strengthened the body of the Church** and who stepped forward to save the day. When their help was needed, these young men were ready, worthy, and willing to respond.

Helaman told Moroni that his 'little force' had given the Nephite army great hopes and much joy' (Alma 56:17). As compared with Helaman's

2,000, today there are nearly 2,000,000 of you in this Church between the ages of 18 and 25.

Imagine then what an army of 2,000,000 chaste, honest, dedicated young men and women filled with the power of God in great glory can do—and must do! There is no greater cause. There is no greater army for righteousness than you.

The Lord needs faithful, articulate, committed men and women who are undaunted by what lies ahead and who are willing to stand up for what is right again and again; who do not doubt what the Lord will do for them; who keep their covenants with exactness; who have decided that, at all costs, they will live on the Lord's side of the line. "

ACKNOWLEDGEMENTS:

As always, I am so very thankful to my loving wife, Janet for all her patience and page by page feedback as this story unfolded.

I am most grateful to both Danielle K. Gleave who I knew as Sister Maddox while serving in the Paris Visitor's center. She provided tireless professional editing feedback from beginning to ending.

I am also grateful to my sister Debbie Frogley Broberg, who, as an educator, provided some final editing and feedback.

After publishing the first edition of this book, a friend, Cherie Green commented that she had combed the book for evidence that the main character, Sam was, in fact, the elusive "Samuel, the Lamanite." What a great idea! After recalculating the years, it was evident to me that climbing the wall, and "casting himself down from the wall, describe the actions of a younger man than someone in the later seventies. So, I added a chapter and adjusted a few earlier elements. Thank you, Cherie!

Made in United States
Orlando, FL
11 December 2024

55366154R10068